Love & Drama: The Root of All Evil

By

Sheena Binkley

Love & Drama: The Root of All Evil
Sheena Binkley

Editor: Crystal Collier
Book Cover: Angel Walker
Formatting by: Sheena Binkley
Published in the United States of America

Acknowledgements

Heavenly Father, thank you for your continuous blessings, You have helped me through so much, even when I don't deserve it. Thank you for giving me the strength and guidance throughout my life's journey, including my journey as an author. I will always be grateful for everything that You have done for me, each and every day.

To my husband, Ethan. We have been through a lot these past few months, so thank you for continuing believing in me. I appreciate it and I appreciate you.

To the people that does support me (you know who you are), thank you so much. When I first started, I had a lot of doubters (and still do), but for the ones who have stuck by me, I would have to say you all are so important to me and I will always be grateful for your love and support.

Laurencia Smith, as always, thank you so much. You have always been a support system for me by being there for me and listening to me when I needed someone to talk to. Just know that I will always be there for you, having that listening ear when needed. Love you, sis!

To my beta readers, thank you so much for taking the time and reading this story. Thank you for the valuable feedback as well as enjoying the story. I truly appreciate it.

Last, but not least, thank you to the readers who have stuck by me and supported me. Words cannot express how much you all mean to me. I appreciate the love you all have always given me and I hope that everyone continue to support me for years to come.

Again, I appreciate it! :-)

Other Books by Sheena Binkley

Available Now:

<u>In Love With My Best Friend series</u>

In Love With My Best Friend (Camille & Trevor)
A Chance at Love (Tia & Charles)
The Wedding Part I (Camille & Trevor)
The Wedding Part II (Tia & Charles)

<u>Love , Life, & Happiness series</u>

Love Unbroken (Riana & Shawn)
Trust Me (Cheryl & Marcus)
Unconditional Love (Britney & Jayden)
The Way We Were (Monica & Donnell)
Love Always (Riana & Shawn)
Redemption (Nathan)
Love, Life, & Happiness Christmas

<u>Something Just Ain't Right series (Hayley & Morgan)</u>

Something Just Ain't Right
Something Just Ain't Right 2
Something Just Ain't Right 3
Just Right (SJAR Novella)

<u>No Other Love series (Kevin, Carla, & Jennifer)</u>

No Other Love
No Other Love 2
No Other Love 3

<u>One Shot With A Baller series (Jayden & Zack)</u>

One Shot With A Baller- The Complete Series

<u>The Love Chronicles series (Andre & Dexter)</u>

The Love Chronicles
Say That You Love Me
How Deep Is Your Love
Love You For Life (Coming Soon)

Into You series
Into You (Vanessa & Mark)
Resisting Temptation (Reece & Troy)

Love, Life, & Happiness: The Lost Story
The Lost Story- Parts 1-3
The Lost Story- Part 4 (Coming Soon)

Reclaiming What Is Mine series (Asia & Bryon)
Reclaiming What Is Mine
Reclaiming What Is Ours (Coming Soon)

Lessons In Love series
Lessons In Love (Trina)

Standalone Books
Our Love (Charlie & Michael)
The Evolution Of Love (Elise, Jared, & Dante)
Love & Drama: The Root Of All Evil (Zuri & Damon)
I'm The Only One You Need (Mika, Devin, & Anthony)
Real Love (Riana & Shawn)
Believe In Love (Cheryl & Marcus)
Lady Guardians: The Ultimate Risk (Raven & Ryan)

Love & Drama: The Root of All Evil (BWWM)

He's a hitman who's trying to change his ways.
She's the good girl that loves to do bad things.
When these two are together, anything is possible.

When Zuri Caldwell meets Damon Baxter at a club five years ago, she never expected for her life to be turned upside down. After having a one-night stand together, she never realized she would be seeing him again, until she sets foot in his classroom.

While they try to stay away, the attraction is still there that the two cannot deny, leading them to have a discreet relationship. That is, until Zuri moves to California for an executive position.

Five years later and she is back in Houston, lost on her luck since she was fired from her job over an event that went extremely wrong. She encounters Damon again, which sparks up old memories. Even though Damon wants her back, Zuri doesn't since she just got over an engagement. However, that doesn't mean she won't sample a little of what he's offering.

The two fall back into a sexual relationship that could prove dangerous since Damon has been living a double life. He tried to leave his old life as a hitman behind, but his past keeps catching up with him, forcing him into doing one last hit. He never wanted to do it, but there's a reason he has to, Zuri. There's one catch though, she has to be involved as well. Mainly because her ex-fiancé is the target.

The two have to find a way to get what the men need without tipping off anyone, including their friends, Zuri's parents, and most of all, her ex. But can the two do it without having their feelings get involved?

Zuri

"Are you ready?"

I glanced at Damon, feeling completely terrified to what we were about to do. He held my hand, squeezing it while his blue eyes stared into mine. I looked behind me, wondering if we were still being chased. Luckily, Damon found a way to get them off of our trail.

He flashed that smile of his that made my pussy wet. This is not the time to be thinking about that, especially when they're people trying to kill us.

"You know I got you, right?"

I nervously nodded. "I know. I trust you."

We heard gunshots as I looked behind me. Damon pulled me to the edge, yelling we have to go. I gave a silent prayer, asking God to keep us safe as I closed my eyes, not wanting to look where I was heading.

"Zuri, let's go!"

I quickly opened them as we jumped off the edge of the cliff, heading towards the rushing waters, hoping we don't die.

From the time I've known Damon, he turned my life upside down. But in the two months that we have reconnected, never did I imagine it would be this crazy. That's why I didn't let him back into my life. Now, I have to wonder did I make the right decision in getting back with him.

I guess I would never know the outcome. Or, will I?

Five Years Earlier…

"Girl, I told you we should have left early. Now, we have to pay."

I looked at my friend, Nicole Easley, and sighed. Leave it to her to worry about being at the club on time. Even though Bases is the new club in the city, I could care less since I didn't even want to go out. She dragged me out since she broke up with her boyfriend, Malik, for the hundredth time, and wanted to celebrate. I'm pretty sure she'll be back with him by the end of the night. They always do.

I looked behind me, wishing I could leave, when someone caught my attention. He was talking with a group of guys when he looked over and stared at me. Our eyes locked as he gave a sexy smile.

"Damn, he's fine," Nicole said.

"I know right," I agreed. I continued to stare as he turned to his friends. He stepped out of line and came over to me, which caught me by surprise. With his porcelain skin, sky blue eyes, and short way black hair, he was even sexier up close as his eyes roamed my body.

"Hey."

"Hey. You know you can't just skip the line. People might start a riot."

"I hardly doubt that. If so, it'll be worth it."

I smiled and he stepped closer to me. "What's your name?"

"Shouldn't I be asking you that?"

"I asked you first."

"Zuri."

"Sexy name, which fits you perfectly."

I looked over at Nicole who was fanning herself. He was still giving that smile, which quickly had me clutching my thighs. He keeps doing that and I might have to do something about it, in other words, do him.

"Let me see if your name fits you."

"Okay. Damon."

I smiled. "It definitely does."

"You think we could talk some more, that is, if your friend doesn't mind."

"Hell no! Go do your thing, girl. I have my eyes on your blonde friend anyway," Nicole said while waving at him.

"That's Chandler, and yes, he's single."

"My kind of man. Excuse me," she said and went over to him.

I smiled. "That's typical of her."

"So, do you do this often? Pick up random guys at clubs?" Damon asked.

I laughed. "I think it's the other way around. You came over and talked to me."

"I couldn't resist. You're sexy as hell."

"You're not so bad yourself."

"I think I'm more than that, especially with how you're looking at me."

He came over to me. The scent of him and his Gucci cologne overcame me, making me even more wet. I didn't think that was possible.

“You want to fuck me right now, don’t you?”

I glanced at him. I couldn’t believe he just said that.

“Aren't you bold?”

“I’m just telling the truth.”

“I’m not that type of girl.”

“No one is ever quite what they seem.”

I glanced at him as I didn’t realize we were near the entrance. The bouncer asked for our IDs, but Damon shook his head. He took my hand as we went out of the line.

“What are you doing?”

“Let’s get to know each other.”

“But my friend…”

“She said she’ll be fine.”

“Yeah, but if we were in the same place. I’m not going anywhere with you.”

“You don’t want to get to know me?”

“You could be a damn killer.”

“Do I look like I could be?”

“A lot of fine looking men were killers.”

“We won’t go far. In fact, we can go to the diner next door.”

I stared at him, wondering if I should. I’d never done this before. I was usually the responsible one. I looked at Nicole, who was encouraging me to go. I put up the peace sign, which was her code to tell me to call if I didn't hear from her within two hours. I didn't think I would be using it for myself.

Damon nodded and we walked to the diner. He looked at me and smiled.

"So, I'm assuming you never done this before."

"Does it look like I have? What are you trying to say?"

"I'm not saying anything. I just assumed because you look nervous. You don't have to be. I'm harmless. Besides, if you didn't want to, you could have said so."

"Yes, I could have, but as you can see, I didn't."

"That's because you want to fuck me."

"Wow, you're cocky."

"I just call it how I see it. Believe me, if you do, then the feelings are mutual."

I blushed as we walked inside. We found the closest booth to sit down and I started to play with my menu. Damon looked ahead as something caught his attention. I looked over and saw three men staring at him. I quickly turned around, wondering what the hell was going on.

"Is everything okay?"

He nodded. "Yeah, everything is cool. You can order something if you want."

"I'm good. Thanks."

We sat in silence for a few minutes before Damon started to ask questions. The two of us got into a conversation about everything from our favorite food, music, even our childhood. After four hours of talking, I didn't even realize that Nicole had called twice.

Damon checked his watch and smiled. “I didn’t realize how late it was.”

“Me either. It was nice to actually have a decent conversation with someone.”

“I’m not sure what guys you’ve been talking to, but I like my women to be sexy and stimulating, which you definitely are. There is one other question I want to ask.”

“What’s that?”

“Have you been with anyone outside your race?”

“Honestly, no.”

“Have you thought about it?”

“I have.”

“If you’re wondering, I’ve been pretty diverse. I think all women are beautiful, so I don’t have a preference.”

I nodded. “I really think I should go. I’m pretty sure Nicole is looking for me. We have classes tomorrow and we shouldn’t be out so late.”

“I do too, but I’m not leaving. In fact, I don’t want the night to end.”

“It’s going to have to.”

“No, it doesn’t. Come home with me.”

“Whoa, what? If you think that I’ll…”

“I’m not thinking that. I just want to get to know you better.”

“Which you have and can another day.”

I got up when he gently grabbed my hand. I stared into those blue eyes of his, being completely hypnotized by them.

“What do you say?”

I slowly nodded, not knowing what the hell I was doing. He got up and put his hand on my waist as we walked out. I hope I don’t regret this.

Damon

I looked at Zuri, who was nervously pulling down her dress. Damn, she's sexy. I really want to know her, but it was hard for me not to touch her or kiss those pouty lips of hers. Her golden brown skin looked soft to touch. I imagined her legs wrapped around me, her eyes staring into mine as I pleasured her. I know it won't happen tonight, but hell, I wished it did.

She pushed her wavy brown hair from her face as she looked at me. "I have to admit, for a college student, you must be doing something since you have this car."

"I just work hard for what I have."

"There's nothing wrong with that. I did tell Nicole where I was heading, so if you try anything, she'll have the cops at your place in a heartbeat."

"She wouldn't know where I stay."

"Trust me, I'll get your address in a few."

I smiled as I pulled into my apartment complex. She looked from the building to me and shook her head.

"Tell me what you do for a living, because no college student has all this. Unless he has rich parents."

"Which I don't. They passed when I was six from a car accident."

Zuri looked sad. "Sorry to hear that."

"It's cool. My uncle was the one who raised me, even when my parents were alive, so I consider him my real parent."

I turned off the ignition and we got out of the car. She looked at me and I guided her to my place. She was still nervous, but hopefully I can loosen her up.

As soon as we walked into my apartment, she was in awe over it. I can understand since I'm 24 and living pretty decent with a luxury apartment and a BMW 328i, but there's a reason for that, which is something Zuri or anyone else would never know.

"Do you sell drugs?" she asked.

"Why is that the first thought that came to mind?"

"Because you're still in college, so you haven't started your career yet. Damn, I'm with a dealer. I knew it! That's what I get for talking to you outside of the club."

"Zuri, stop. I don't push drugs. In fact, I never touched the stuff."

She folded her arms across her chest and gave a stern look. "So, how are you paying for this? Even student loans couldn't cover this."

"I have a great job with incentives, that's all."

"And what is this line of work that you do?"

"I work for a prominent figure in the city. I take orders from him. In fact, he paid for everything that I have."

"That really helps. You know what, I think I'm going to go," she said, heading to the door. I went over to her and held her in my arms. She stared into my eyes, which I knew was the breaking point for her. It seemed as if she was in a trance when she stared into them.

"Please, don't go."

"Why should I stay? I've only known you for a few hours and I still don't know you. So give me a reason as to why I should still be here."

What she said that for, because I have a million reason for her to stay. I guided her to the wall as my body pressed against hers. My hand gently touched her thigh, as she shivered.

"That's one reason. Let me give you another one," I whispered and reached for her lips. As soon as I kissed her, my body had a mind of its own. She spread her legs while I slowly kissed her neck. She slightly moaned and my hand went to her ass. Damn, she has a nice ass.

"Damon, we shouldn't do this."

"Why not? You and I are both attracted to each other, so there's nothing wrong with what we're doing."

"I don't do one-night stands."

"Who said it has to be one night?"

She stared at me while her hand was on my chest. I pulled it up to my lips and gently sucked each finger. She sighed, pulling away from me and took off my shirt. I pulled her to me as we walked over to the couch, taking off each other's clothes. I sat down and she straddled me, her lips leading a trail of kisses down my chest. My hands caressed her, lining her up so I could feel her warmness against me. I leaned back as she kissed my earlobe.

"There's something I've been wanting to do since I first saw you."

"And what is that?"

"I can show you better than I can tell you."

She bit her lip as my tongue slowly went between her breasts, licking her golden brown skin that I've been wanting to touch for hours. She gave a heavenly sigh as I continued to seduce her, softly kissing her from her navel to her thighs. I sat her up as I laid down on the couch. I leaned her body forward, placing her clit to my lips. As soon as we connected, she softly moaned while putting her hands on the wall to steady herself. She spread herself for me as my tongue went to work on her. Damn, she tasted good. So good that I could eat her out for hours.

I grabbed her thighs, bringing her closer to me while she rode me. She titled her head back, her tits bouncing while her moans increased. She started repeating my name, and I knew then she was reaching her breaking point.

I flicked my tongue while grabbing her ass, making her body move in a rapid pace. She leaned back, touching herself as I continued licking her.

"Fuck, I'm cummmmminnng!" she screamed as her juices went all over me. To me, getting a woman off so good that she's squirting is a fucking turn on for me. That meant I was doing my damn job.

She got off of me and stared into my eyes.

"You definitely showed me."

I laughed as she came to me and licked herself off of my lips.

"That's what I'm talking about."

She began to look nervous, which was strange to me since she just showed all of herself a while ago. I stared into her eyes, becoming mesmerized by them.

"Don't hold back to how you feel, Zuri. If you want me, then feel free to take control. Besides, you spoiled me with that performance you just gave, so I have to see that again."

"Oh really."

"Yes, but this time, I *need* to be inside of you."

She smiled and I pulled her off the couch. I walked us over to the kitchen counter and sat her down. She looked into my eyes while my hand went to her clit. My fingers dipped inside of her as she leaned back. She was ready, but I needed her to say it.

"Please, Damon."

"Please, what?"

"Stop teasing me and fuck me."

"Say it again."

"Damn it, Damon, I need you inside of me. Now!"

I smiled as I grabbed a condom from the kitchen drawer. I have them everywhere for when the mood strikes. She gave me a strange look, but I changed that once I kissed her.

"Are you really ready?"

"Yes."

I slid it on and stared at her. She put her arms around me as her legs went around my waist. I pulled her to the edge of the counter as I slowly went inside of her. We continued to look at each other as I began moving in her. Her hands went down my back while I slightly leaned against her, spreading her legs so she could get a better feel of me. She grabbed my ass, her nails digging across my flesh, which made me go deeper in her. Her body shook as mine was going out of control. I didn't think this would happen this soon. I was only with her for a short time and I was already addicted. I don't know if that was a good sign or a desperate one.

She couldn't even say a word, but her eyes told it all when I knew she was cumming again. They were glossed over, as her body shook again. She wiggled her hips, as her body spasmed. She wanted me to cum too as she leaned against me. She moved on my dick as I looked into her eyes. I wanted her to see me cum. She couldn't take her eyes off of me as I took her hand and slid it down my chest. I leaned her against the counter, still staring at her, as my lips went to her ear, whispering "I'm cumming" while her body was going off again. She was cumming with me, which was something I never experienced with anyone before.

We glanced at each other, not wanting to move from our position as I touched her face. I knew right then that this was going to be more than just a one-night stand.

“I don’t know if I can leave you.”

She looked at me, wondering what I meant. “Why would you say that?”

“Because I don’t think I can.”

“This was just a fuck, right?” she asked.

“Maybe, but you and I know that it can be much more. That’s if you want it to be.”

“I don’t know. We just met.”

“Like I said before, it doesn’t have to be one night.”

I pulled her up and held her in my arms. She didn’t know what to say as I took her to the bedroom. I laid her down on the bed and I laid down beside her.

“What are you doing?” she asked.

I didn’t say anything as I pulled her to me. She took a deep breath as she laid her head down on my chest and sighed.

“What do you think?”

“It's too soon to tell, but maybe I need more convincing.”

I turned her face to me and gave her a passionate kiss. I don't know how she got to me so soon, but I already knew there will be more between us. I just hope she will know that soon.

Zuri

I can't believe I did that! I'm still in shock that I slept with a complete stranger. I'm not going to lie, it was good. Damn, it was good. But just because it was doesn't excuse the fact that I fucked someone that I just met not too long ago. That was tacky and nasty, and those two things are not me.

Once I got over the initial shock of my actions, I tried to leave Damon's place. While I was in the middle of putting my dress on, he picked me up, put me on the top of his dresser and ate me out until I was too weak to move. This guy was perfect. He's sexy, funny, and can make my pussy cum more in one night compared to my entire life. Regardless of all that, I couldn't be with him. That's why after we had sex for the third time, I grabbed my clothes and snuck out while he was asleep. Now it was the next day and I was walking into my principles of economics class exhausted, but a little happy, all because of the night I had. It was well worth it.

I sat down in a seat besides Nicole as she gave me a smirk. "Nice to see you this morning. I didn't think you were going to make it to class since you were out all night."

"I did come back to the apartment. I guess you had a good night too."

"It was good. Chandler took me back home, kissed me and left. He was the perfect gentlemen. I can only imagine what you were up to, you little hoe."

"Does it look like I did anything? Damon and I just talked the entire night."

"Sure, so I guess you didn't see all those hickeys on the left side of your neck. I guess he was already branding his territory."

I quickly pulled out my compact and opened to the mirror. Sure enough, there were a bunch of marks on my neck that I didn't even realize were there.

"Damn it."

"Shit, he must have put it on you good. But I'm surprised at you, you never get down on the first encounter."

I sighed. "I know, it just happened."

"It's those eyes. Trust me, you did the right thing. Too bad you won't see him again."

I glanced at her and she shrugged. She's probably right. Even if there was a chance of us seeing each other again, I kind of ruined us getting together since I left his place in the middle of the night.

I was about to pull out my iPad when the doors swung open and someone walked in. Someone that I was not expecting at all.

"Good morning, class. How is everyone today?" he said as he put down his briefcase and looked at us. He looked into the crowd and automatically spotted me sitting in the second row. He couldn't take his eyes off of me as he mumbled shit. Several students turned to see what he was staring at. I quickly looked into my backpack, pretending I was looking for something.

Damon cleared his throat before going to the projector. "My name is Damon Baxter and I'll be filling in for Professor Thomas for the remainder of the semester."

Nicole giggled. "Damn, you fucked the professor."

I punched her shoulder as several people turned to stare at me. Damon looked at me again before going to the projector to start class. I was already feeling guilty over what I'd done, but to know I slept with an instructor, really made me feel like a slut. I lowered myself in my seat, praying that class would be over soon.

***

Once Damon announced that class was over, I was the first at the door.

“Miss Caldwell, may I see you for a moment, please?”

Nicole nudged me and I sighed. “Go talk to your man.”

“Shut up.”

“I want the full details of your ‘talk’.”

I nudged her again and her overdramatic ass collided with another student. I shook my head and walked over to his desk. He waited until the last person left, and closed and locked the door. I stared at him as he walked over to me, looking as good as he wanted to.

“Why did you leave last night? I was going to make you breakfast.”

“You know why, and it’s a good thing I did. You’re a fucking teacher!”

“I’m a T.A., and Professor Thomas is my mentor. He asked me to fill in while he has surgery.”

“You should have mentioned that to me.”

“I sort of did. He’s running for mayor and working here does pay my bills. Well, some of them.”

“So, you lied to get into my pants.”

“Technically, you weren’t wearing pants. You enjoyed every kiss, touch, lick, and stroke that I was giving you, so don’t even stand here wishing it didn’t happen. You probably want it to happen right now.”

"You're delusional."

"And you're lying to yourself," he said and came closer to me. My body quickly responded, which I hated. Just the thought of him touching me again had me on edge. He's dangerous for me, because once I knew I would give in, I would be hooked.

"I see I left my mark on you."

"Yeah, which I don't like. I don't like when guys try to do that. I'm no one's territory."

"It wasn't even like that. I was enjoying you and got carried away. You know how to please a man," he said while grabbing my hips. He sat me down on the desk and wrapped his arms around me.

"What are you doing? We can't be together, especially now."

"Why not?"

"You know Kennedy has a strict policy about professor/student relationship."

"I'm not a professor, so that rule doesn't apply to us."

"We can't do this."

"We can and stop being scared. You want me just as much as I want you. Stop fighting it and let things be."

He unbuttoned my jeans, pulling them down to my feet. He grabbed me, pulling my lips while I kicked off my sandals and jeans. He took me off the desk and leaned me against the wall. I pulled down his jeans, seeing him spring to life, which had me grinning.

"See, you can't resist me."

He kissed me while sliding himself inside of me. His tongue was grazing my ear while his hands palmed my ass.

"You are on the pill, right?"

I slowly nodded while moaning. Normally, I don't let anyone go in me without a condom, but with how he was hitting my walls, I couldn't do anything else but moan.

"You know you can't resist this," he whispered, and I unraveled. I couldn't resist it or him. I haven't known him for twenty-four hours and I was already in too deep with him.

My fingernails clawed his back and he went in me even harder. Yes, I could get used to this.

"Yes, Damon!"

He leaned into me and my body spasmed, feeling the sensation that left my body satisfied, but craving more. He breathed against me, holding me tight, not wanting to let me go.

"I wasn't expecting that."

"I was. I knew I'd see you again."

"How will this work?"

"We have to keep it a secret. It'll make things interesting, don't you think?"

"I thought you said the rule doesn't apply to you?"

"It sort of does, but I'll take a risk for you."

"You hardly know me."

"Which I hope will change."

He put my feet on the ground, which had me a little woozy. He held me again and kissed my forehead.

“I want to get to know you, Zuri Caldwell. That is, if you’ll let me.”

I smiled. “I do.”

He smiled. “Cool. You think you can handle being in this class without wanting to jump me?”

I laughed. “I can control my urges. That’s something you should be asking yourself.”

“You know I can’t. I could barely talk when I saw you and thought about all the things we did last night. That’s why I can’t let you go.”

I nodded, wondering what I’ll do. How could I immediately put my trust in someone that I just met? But when I looked into his eyes, I realized there was something about him that put me at ease, making me feel safe. That’s why I’ll let go of my doubts and give things a try with him.

Damon

Five Months Later…

"Hey Uncle Julian. I'm fine. Everything is great."

I looked at the clock, wondering when I would receive the phone call I've been waiting on for two hours. It was an important message from my boss telling me when to do an assignment for him.

While my uncle kept talking, I was looking at pictures of Zuri and me, wondering if I'll see her tonight. Since that day in class, the two of us decided to give things a try, which turned out really great. I never imagined that I would be in a relationship with someone I had a one-night stand with, but she makes me happy. I could see myself spending the rest of my life with her, which I've never seen in any other woman. That's pretty special.

Although our relationship is private, the only ones who know about it is my uncle, my friends, and Nicole. Hopefully we can keep it that way until Zuri graduates, which was in one more month, then we can finally go public.

"Zuri's great, Unc. We're pretty happy. I know that it's a shock to you that I'm with someone for so long, but I can't see myself with anyone else. And no, I'm not pussy whipped. Maybe just a little, but I think I'm falling in love with her. I know, Unc, but let me go, my baby's here. Okay, bye."

I looked through the window as she was patiently waiting for me to answer the door. I opened it and she walked in, giving me a sensual kiss.

"Not that I'm complaining, but what was that for?"

"Just for being you, and I have some exciting news."

"Lay it on me."

"I got the position at Randall Promotions. You're looking at their new event planner to the stars."

"That's great baby. Congrats!" I said and pulled her to me for a hug. She gave a slow sigh, as I wondered what was wrong.

"You don't sound too happy though, so what's the catch?"

"Although the company is here, the position is in L.A."

I stared at her as she went to the couch. "They're expanding the company and what better way to do it than in L.A."

"You know that won't be a problem, right? I mean, we can make it work."

Zuri sighed. "That's the thing, Damon, I don't think we can. Even though I want to, we both know long distance relationships are doomed to fail. What if one of us meets someone else?"

"I won't. I'm perfectly satisfied with being with you."

"But you'll get lonely. You can easily talk to another woman. You did with me."

"Yes, how our relationship started was a bit crazy, but it worked. Six months later and we're still together."

"But look at everything we had to go through to make it work. We had to lie and sneak around to be together."

"Which we don't have to do in a few weeks. Why end it now?"

"Because I have a career to think about. If the situation was reversed, you would do the same thing."

"I would, but I would keep the relationship going. I wouldn't let that get in the way of what we have."

Zuri sighed. "Damon..."

"Do you want to see other people?"

"It's not that…"

"Then what is it? Are you tired of me? If so, then maybe we shouldn't be together."

"I'm just giving you a heads up so you can move on with your life."

"Are you fucking kidding me? Just a few days ago you wanted to be with me, and now you don't. Go ahead and find another dude to pick up and bang on the first night."

Zuri laughed. "You're an asshole."

"You used to like that, didn't you?"

I looked out through the window and saw two guys dressed in black approach the house. I looked from them to Zuri as one of them pulled out a gun and aimed it at her.

"Get down!!" I yelled and grabbed my gun from my waistband. I started firing through the glass as it shattered outside. They continued firing while I did the same, hitting one of them in the neck.

"Oh my God!" Zuri screamed.

I told her to get behind the couch as I continued, hoping I could take out his partner, which I did, shooting him in the head. I looked around my place and sighed.

"Muthafuckers."

I went over to Zuri, who was still behind the couch with her knees to her chest. She had a scared look on her face as I looked into her eyes.

"Are you okay?"

"What the hell was that? What did you get yourself into?"

"Please, let me explain…"

"Explain what? I just witnessed a fucking shootout with you killing them both!"

"There's a reason for that."

"I don't know if I want to hear it."

"If you do, then you'll understand. I'm a hitman."

Zuri quickly got up and tried to go to the door, but I stopped her.

"Wait! Don't go out there in case anyone else is outside."

"I'm not going to be here with you! You lied to me."

"I never lied to you. I just didn't tell you."

"Don't try to justify your actions. How long have you been doing this?"

"For two years."

Zuri shook her head. "So that's how you got this place, huh? Sure not on your T.A. salary or being an errand boy."

"Yes, that's how I make a living, but I'm trying to leave the business. I just thought I could do it before you found out."

"Wow, that's what I get for being with someone on the first night. You just never know who you're with."

"Zuri, I didn't tell you because I wanted to protect you. If anyone would have known about you, you could have been in danger."

"I would have been in danger regardless, Damon! Look what happened."

"I know that, but…"

"I think it's a good thing that we're ending things now."

"Baby, don't walk out on me. You know we can make things work."

I pulled her to me and she tried to push away, but I wouldn't let her.

"Let me go, Damon."

"Despite everything, you want to be with me."

"And why is that? Because you can fuck me good? We've only known each other for six months. What do we possibly know about each other to make things work?"

I pulled her up and she responded by wrapping her legs around me. I took her into the bedroom, hoping that I could change her mind about ending things.

***

The bright light from the sun was creeping into my room as I opened one eye. I quickly closed it, hating that it was morning and I had to get up for class. I moved my hand over to touch Zuri, but felt nothing but sheets. I was fully awake, seeing that she was gone. I sighed, seeing a note was laying on the pillow. I read it, balled it up, and hit my fist against the wall. After everything that has happened, she still left. I got up, realizing the day wasn't going to stop.

Neither was my life.

Zuri

Five Years Later…

“Hi, Mom.”

“Hey Zuri. I was wondering if your flight landed safely.”

“Of course it did. I’m heading to Nicole’s now.”

“You know you can stay with your dad and me, sweetie. We know you’re in a tough position right now, so we’ll help anyway we can.”

I sighed. There was no way I was staying with my parents. I was already feeling like a fucking failure as it is.

“Thanks, but no thanks. Nicole is expecting me.”

“Well, try to at least stop by the house, okay?”

“Will do. Love you.”

“Love you too.”

I hung up and sighed again. Five years ago, I was riding high with a great career, living the good life in L.A. My job took me to various places, from London to Paris, and even Jamaica. Now, my dream job has turned into a nightmare, due in part to me making a stupid decision.

One night at a huge event, I got drunk and took topless pictures of myself, which was bad enough. To make matters even worse, I made a sex tape with my ex-fiancé at the event, which one of my co-workers discovered and sent it to every employee. Not only was I the talk of the office, but I was fired and kicked out of the building. Yep, my event planning days are over.

I went up to Nicole's house, trying to decide if I wanted to stay with her. I knew she wouldn't judge me, but her life has done a complete 180. No longer was she the party girl that I remembered. Instead, she's a consultant with a PR firm, married, and has a one-year-old son. Although I'm happy for her, there was one reason why I didn't want to stay with her.

She's married to Damon's best friend, Chandler.

I took a deep breath, hoping Chandler wasn't there. I rang the doorbell and it quickly opened as Nicole pulled me into the house and hugged me.

"My bestie! I can't believe you're back! I missed you."

"I missed you too. Too bad it's not under better circumstances."

Nicole sighed. "I know, but you brought that on yourself getting drunk and going buck wild at an event. Only the guests do that, not the help."

"Well, I learned my lesson. Now, where should I put my things?"

I looked over and saw Chandler along with the man that I've been dreading to see. I had to steady myself at the sight of him. Time has definitely been good to him as his blue eyes stared intensely into mine. His clean-shaven face now had a bit of a scruff as his black hair was neatly cut. Damn, he looked good.

He stood up and walked over to me, flashing that smile of his that always made my panties drop. I seriously needed to control my damn self and focus on getting my life in order, not wanting to sex him right in the living room.

"Hey Zuri."

"Damon."

I glanced over at Chandler and Nicole, who both had smiles on their faces, before leaving the room. I stood shocked that they would leave us alone.

“You looked scared to be alone with me. You shouldn’t be.”

“Who said that I was?”

“Because of your eyes. They always give away your emotions.”

He was so close to me that I could smell his cologne. He looked into my eyes and sighed.

"I should be pissed at you for walking out on me, but I think you’re getting what you deserve with your amateur video.”

I smirked and he laughed. “You never did that with me, but if you did, you know I wouldn’t have broadcast it like your ex did.”

“He didn’t send out the video. And how did you even know about that?”

“It was on social media. Well, not the actual video, but your selfies definitely were. I remember those tits anywhere.”

“You really are being an ass right now.”

“How am I being the ass when you embarrassed yourself and lost your job? That’s not my fault.”

“But you’re happy it happened since I walked out on you.”

“Despite what you think, I would never want anything to happen to you. You should know that.”

I walked over to the couch so I wouldn’t stand so close to him. He followed and sat by me.

“Have you dated anyone else?”

He glanced at me. “I talked to some girls, but I didn’t pursue anything. So yes, I slept with a few, if that’s what you’re asking.”

“I wasn’t asking that.”

“Whatever, Zuri. Besides, I wasn’t the one that was engaged to someone. By the way, he was a bitch anyway.”

“How mature.”

“He’s a bitch ass who relied on his parents’ money. How did you meet him anyway?”

“Why do you care? We broke up.”

“Just asking.”

“Moving on. Did you quit your other job or you doing double duty?”

He nodded. “I quit two years ago. I’m fully legit with being an instructor.”

I smiled. “That’s great.”

“I said I wanted to leave, but you still looked as if I wasn’t going to.”

“I didn’t like the fact that you lied to me. You left out that you kill people for a living.”

“It not like they were good people, so I was doing society a favor.”

“That still doesn’t make it right. Besides the two that you killed, how many more people did you kill?”

“Does it matter?”

“Yes, it does.”

“Over twenty.”

I pulled away from him and he sighed. "Listen, my boss asked me to do these things so he wouldn't get his hands dirty. They were guys who had done bad things, and that was their punishment."

"Who made you God, Damon? That wasn't your place to punish anyone!"

"It was my job to do it. Maybe I did regret it, but the damage is done now. All that matters is that I'm no longer doing it. I wanted to change my ways, and I did it, so be glad about that."

"What made you do it though? Was it the money, or were you forced to do it? What was it?"

"That I can't answer, Zuri. Maybe one day I can, but not right now."

I held up my hands. "Whatever, Damon."

"Why are you so mad? You walked out on us, so why should I give you any type of explanation?"

"So, you're going to keep throwing that in my face?"

"Just like you are with me being a hitman. We all make mistakes in our lives, but sometimes we're given a second chance. That was mine, and you will have yours too."

"I know I will, it's just going to take some time. I'm pretty much blacklisted by every firm in the United States, so I might have to consider going into another field."

"When there's a will, there's a way, Zuri. You'll get back to where you were."

I smiled as he placed a hand on my thigh. His fingers slowly caressed my skin, sending waves through me. I hate my body right now. There's always going to be a part of me that wants him. I don't think that connection will go away.

"Why didn't you come to Nicole's wedding?"

I sighed. I talked to her before her wedding to let her know I couldn't attend. I just didn't want to, especially since Damon was Chandler's best man. Instead, I was there through Skype, watching it and regretting not being there. I know no matter what Nicole said, it hurt her that I wasn't there.

"I couldn't face you."

He sighed. "You hurt Nicole. She still talks about it. You couldn't put your feelings for me aside to support her? I'm surprised she let you stay here after what you pulled."

"That's none of your concern."

"She's Chandler's wife, so it is my concern."

I rolled my eyes. "I know I hurt Nicole, but we talked it out and we're fine, so you don't have to worry about it."

"If you say so. Understand this, you can't run or hide from me because I'll be right here, so you're going to be seeing me all the time."

"You don't think I know that. That's one of the reasons why I didn't want to return."

Damon pulled me to him, forcing me to stare at him. "Eventually, you're going to remember those times we had and how I turned your body out. You know you'll be back in my bed soon."

"You're a cocky muthafucker."

"What's with the language? You must know it's true."

"You're still cocky."

"Which you love, baby. Just admit it."

I got up and picked up my suitcase. “I’m going to my room, wherever that is.”

“You need any help? I can definitely help with undressing you.”

I gave him the finger, and he smiled.

“I preferred if you did.”

I turned around and went down the hallway. A smile slowly crossed my lips at our little exchange. I hate to admit it, but he was definitely right.

Damon

I watched Zuri walk away and moaned. Damn, I missed her. More than I wanted to admit. It has been five years since she walked out on me, and she's done everything to avoid seeing me, including missing her best friend's wedding.

I was heading to the door when my phone rang. I pulled it from my pocket and glanced at it, wondering if I should answer it. I haven't seen this number in years, so it was definitely a surprise.

I ignored it, but a few seconds later, they called again. I sighed, walked outside to my car, and answered it.

"You know you shouldn't ignore people's calls, Damon."

"I can, especially if it's you. What do you want, Milo?"

"Just seeing how things were going. How's life as a professor treating you?"

"Cut the bullshit and tell me what you want."

"I need to see you in twenty."

"I'm not meeting you. I've been out of the business for two years now, so whatever you have going on, I don't want any part of."

"You might want to if you want that pretty girl still alive."

"What?"

"You heard me. That girl that you were talking to. If I remember her name, it's Zuri, right?"

"What the hell does she have to do with what you have going?"

"Come meet me and I'll tell you."

"You better tell me."

"Hudson Avenue in ten minutes. Don't be late."

Before I could say anything else, he hung up.

"Fuck!" I said, punching the steering wheel. I looked across the street and saw a black SUV parked. I shook my head and started up my car, wondering what the hell was going on.

I reached Hudson Avenue in the allowed time, seeing another black SUV sitting on the under path. I got out of the car and rushed over to it. I knocked on the window and the door opened.

"Nice to see you, Damon."

"I wish I could say the same, Milo. Now, what the fuck is going on?"

"Get in. We're going for a ride."

I stood there, delaying any time I had because I wasn't getting in the car with him.

His bodyguard, Patrick, grabbed me and shoved me inside, and I fell to the floor.

"You were coming one way or the other. Let's roll."

His driver nodded and we started to move.

"I wish we were meeting under better circumstances, but this is business."

"I told you I'm out."

"Are you really? I'm sure that teaching doesn't pay shit."

"It suits me just fine."

"Well, as I mentioned on the phone, that girl of yours will make you come back."

"Which I'm wondering why she is involved."

"Because she's the reason why we need you for this. Besides, you're being the best at it. She can lead you to the person in question."

I looked confused as Patrick threw a manila envelope at me. I opened it, seeing pictures of Zuri and a man who I saw in countless pictures that Nicole shared.

"This is Zuri's ex."

"Exactly. Tyrik O'Neal is the son of the most notable crime boss in the city, Malcolm O'Neal. We have been at odds over our territories for years now. We tried to form an alliance, but he fucked that up by bringing some of his thugs to my area, taking out a few of my men. Since he wants to play dirty, then I'll do the same, but I'm going deeper by taking out one of his family."

"Whoa, what the hell has he done? You said you would never drag family into your shit."

"Yes, I did say that, but he crossed the line after I tried to be nice. He shouldn't have bit the hand that fed his ass."

"What made you want to make a deal with him anyway?"

"You don't need to know that. What I need for you to do is take him out."

"Ask your new man, because I'm not in this."

"Even if your girl is involved?"

"She's no longer with him, so she shouldn't be involved."

"That's where you're wrong, my friend. Zuri has a lot of ties with him and she could be our go-to girl to get his whereabouts. I need her in this. That's why I need you to be a part of it. If neither of you are on board with this, then you'll both be killed. Plain and simple."

"You're bluffing."

"You really want to try me, Damon? I may have other people do my dirty work, but I can get down like the rest of them, so don't push me."

"You have another agenda behind this, don't you?"

"That you'll never know. So, I need an answer by tonight. If you have the wrong one, then don't be surprise at what will happen to you or that pretty girl of yours. It could be anywhere. At your place, your friend's home, Uncle Julian's. Hell, even your car. It might even be at Zuri's parents'. Lovely people they are. Let's see what they're up to now," he said as he pulled out his phone. He hit a button and it went to a screen of them watching TV. I leaned back in the seat and he smiled.

"Or I can always get my answer now."

"Why would you drag innocent people in this?"

"No one is innocent if they're involved with you. Anyone that crosses your path is fair game. So, what is your answer?"

"I'll do it and get Zuri on board."

"Great answer, Damon. We'll be in touch."

I sighed as the SUV stopped and Patrick opened the door and kicked me out. I looked at them, wondering what the hell they're doing.

"You're throwing me out here?"

"You better be glad it wasn't in the fucking Carson River. Now get your ass out of my face!" Milo yelled and Patrick slammed the door.

I looked around me, wondering how I was going to get back to my car. But with what Milo just stressed, it probably was best if I left it there.

I pulled out my phone, hoping the number I had was still the same.

"What do you want, Damon?"

"I need your help, Zuri."

Zuri

After Damon called me, I wasn't going to pick him up, but my conscience told me I should, so I borrowed Nicole's car and found his location, which was at a diner. I didn't know what the hell was going on, but with Damon, anything was possible.

Once I found him, he asked me to take him to Hudson Avenue to get his car. He wanted me to follow him to the nearest mechanic to check out his car for any suspicious devices. I really didn't want to know what that was about.

When the mechanic gave him the okay, he asked for me to go back to his place so we could talk. I didn't want to, but he said it was urgent, and he didn't need anyone else to know, so I dropped Nicole's car back at her place and left with him.

Once we walked in, a shrew of memories overcame me as I walked around. Except for a few portraits and a new TV, everything was still the same, which made me a little emotional.

"Bringing back memories for you, isn't it?"

"Yeah, it is. So what was so urgent for me to come by?"

"I need to talk about us."

"There's nothing to talk about."

"Zuri, from the time that we've been apart, have you thought about me at least once?"

"Evidently I didn't, if I was engaged to another man."

"That doesn't mean anything. You could have been with him, but were thinking about me touching you, kissing you, making you feel good every time you're with me."

"Are you that desperate for me to be with you?"

"Baby, I can have any woman I want. You're the woman I want to be with, but like you said, you didn't feel the same way."

"It wasn't like that, Damon."

"Then what was it? Please don't say because I'm white."

"You know it's not, even though my parents never knew about you."

"That's obvious."

"There were a few reasons to why I ended things, but that's in the past."

"Which we never talked about."

"Damon, please!"

He saw the pleading look I was giving him, realizing there was more to what happened. He nodded, finally realizing he needed to leave the situation alone. Although it has been five years, I still couldn't talk about it.

"I won't push you, but eventually, you're going to have to tell me the truth."

"When I do, you'll definitely know."

"Zuri, I just want you to be honest with me. If something did happen then you can tell me whenever you're ready to, okay?"

"Thank you."

"Since you're here, you want to have some dinner, maybe talk some more about the good old days."

I smiled. "I don't know if I should."

"Why? Scared to be alone with me?"

I put my hand on his chest as I looked at him. He pushed some hair from my face, staring into my eyes as I was quickly losing control. I couldn't resist those damn eyes of his. They were like a fucking drug that I couldn't shake off.

He slowly pulled me to him as his lips were on my neck. Why did I get caught back into this? I wasn't trying to, but I couldn't help it.

He lowered his head to kiss me, which had me horny and ready. That was a done deal for me. His hand was rubbing my clit as we went over to the couch. I know I'm going to regret this, especially after what I've done. But for a moment, I wanted to erase my mistakes and be with him.

Damon

"What are you thinking about?"

Zuri glanced at me with a shy smile while putting up the blanket she had over her. I slowly pulled it from her, seeing that beautiful body of hers. She laid down on the pillow and sighed.

"I can't believe I'm here with you."

"I told you you'll be back in my bed."

"Cocky muthafucker."

"Say it all you want, but you still like it."

She smiled. "Maybe I do. I missed you."

"If you missed me, you wouldn't have been engaged to another man."

"That was because I felt I had lost you, especially after what I'd done."

"Which you never told me."

"I meant walking away from you."

"You were talking about something else, but like I said, you'll tell me when the time is right."

"I'm sure you know that I asked Nicole about you."

"I know. Chandler can't hold water, so I got all my news from him."

"Figured. He always had a guilty look on his face when I Skyped Nicole."

I stared at her, not believing she was here with me. I would be even more relaxed if I didn't have to tell her about Milo.

"Baby, I have to tell you something."

"What?"

"I saw my old boss earlier today. That's where I was when you picked me up."

"Why did you meet up with him?"

"I was forced to. I have to do a job for him."

"But aren't you out of the business? Why is he asking you to do it?"

"Because he wants the best. And because of my connection with the target."

Zuri looked confused as I took a moment to speak. "Do you know your ex is the son of a crime boss in the city, Malcolm O'Neal?"

"Why would I know that? Tyrik mentioned he was a prominent figure, but never discussed what he does. He was one of the most important clients at Randall. That was also the party I went buck wild at."

I smiled and Zuri shoved me. "Anyway, Malcolm and my former boss, Milo, had some sort of alliance, but it failed when Malcolm tried to use it against Milo to move into his territory. Since he did that, Milo doesn't trust him, so he figured since he took down some of his men…"

"He's going to do the same to him, but on a deeper level. Tyrik's the target."

I nodded.

"Wow, I hope you didn't agree to it. Although Tyrik is a jerk, he doesn't deserve to be killed."

"I have to do it."

"You have a choice, Damon."

"Not when it comes to you. Milo threatened to harm you if I didn't. In fact, since you know Tyrik, he wants you involved."

"Wait, what? Are you serious?"

"I wish I wasn't. If you don't agree, then you won't be the only one in danger. Everyone we know will be, including your parents."

"What! How did they know who they are?"

"Probably because of Tyrik. He showed a video of them, Zuri, so he knows where they stay."

She sat up in the bed and gave a scared look. "What in the hell you got me in, Damon? Bad enough you fucked me before even telling me this!"

"Even if I would have told you before, it still wouldn't have erased what we did. Anyway, whether we want to or not, we're both involved in this, so we have to work together to protect ourselves and our loved ones."

"I can't believe you, Damon. I can't be involved in this. I wouldn't know what to do or how to contact Tyrik. I haven't talked to him since what happened."

"Well, you better find a way, because Milo is out for blood. If we don't deliver, then we're both screwed."

"Who's to say I want to do this? I can always warn my parents and Nicole about what's going on."

"That would be the stupidest thing you could do. He's been watching you, and don't think for a second he's not watching us now."

I got up from the bed and looked out at the window. Sure enough, that same black SUV that was at Nicole and Chandler's, was parked across from my place. I motioned for her to come over to the window and gave her a convinced look.

"That same SUV was at Nicole and Chandler's before I spoke with Milo. Once you leave here, he's going to follow you. He probably has a couple of men watching your parents' every move, so I suggest you do what you need to do to keep them safe."

"How could you do this?"

"I didn't do anything, Zuri. You would have been in this regardless since you were involved with Tyrik. I'm in this because of you, so now, we have to help each other. So, are you in, Z?"

She stared at me and nodded. "Whatever we have to do, then I'm in."

I tried to put my arm around her, but she ignored me and went to pick up her clothes. I went over to her while she was trying to leave.

"So you're going to ignore me now?"

"What do you expect, Damon? You're right, I probably would still be in some shit because of Tyrik. I feel as if my life has been a roller coaster these past few years, and it's only because of my stupid choices."

"Which you're learning from. There's no point in beating yourself up about it. Just do what you can so we can both get out of this mess."

I tried to touch her again, but she pushed away from me.

"Don't touch me," she whispered. She picked up her bag before going to the door.

"I'll catch a cab."

"No, I'll drive you."

"Just leave me alone, Damon!"

Before I could even stop her, a loud boom went through the window, causing both of us to drop down to the floor. A round of shots was going off as someone was firing at us. I pulled Zuri away from the window as I tried to grab my gun from underneath the armchair. I had that in case any shit went down; case in point, right now.

I started firing off as someone was trying to break the door down. I grabbed another gun from underneath the couch and gave it to Zuri. She freaked out, which was not the time for that.

"I don't know how to shoot a gun!"

"Here's your chance now!"

The door flew open and two guys ran in. I immediately shot one of them in the throat, causing him to fall down on the ground. The other guy was going to Zuri, and I was trying to get her to shoot.

"Damn it Zuri, shoot him!"

I knew she was scared, but she had to before both of us were taken out.

She quickly aimed the gun at him as he was going to her. She fired three shots at him, one hit him in the foot. He fell down on the ground as I went over to him with my gun aimed to his chest.

"Now muthafucker, who sent you here? Was it Milo?"

"I'm not saying."

"I'm the one who has a gun aimed at you, so you better start talking."

“You’re going to have to shoot me first.”

“Fair enough,” I said, as the gun went off, hitting him in the chest. I shot him two more times to make sure he was dead. Every time the gun went off, Zuri jumped. I sighed, knowing this would scar her, but I had to do it.

I went over to her to make sure she was okay. She didn’t want to look at me as I turned her to face me.

“I know that was hard for you, but you did good.”

“What was this? Some fucking test to see how I’ll be.”

“I don’t know, but it looks as if it was. I think Milo was trying to see if I was still capable of killing and if you were fit for doing this.”

"All of this is crazy!”

“I know, Zuri, that’s why we need to stick together on this. No turning against each other, especially not now.”

She slowly nodded and I grabbed my phone, about to call Milo, when he walked into my house. He started clapping as I gave him a pissed off look.

“Nice work, Baxter.”

“You’re a sick son of a bitch to do this!”

“You knew I had to. I had to see if you were still capable of being the best, and you proved me right, yet again. Consider yourself proud of what you’ve done.”

“You’re sick.”

“And you changed, personality wise anyway. I guess she had something to do with you going soft,” he said while staring at Zuri.

"She had nothing to do with it. I was just tired of living a double life. Now, I have to get dragged back into something that's not even my fault."

"Stop your bitching, Baxter. Once you do what I asked, then you can go back to being a soft ass."

"Who were the men I killed?"

"They were my men, of course, but they weren't cut out for this, so I found a way to get rid of them."

"That's cruel," Zuri mumbled.

"Ah, we haven't properly introduced ourselves. I'm Milo, and you are one very beautiful woman," he said as he tried to take her hand for a kiss. She pushed away from him as I stepped in between the two.

"Leave her alone."

"For someone who said you weren't together, you sure are protective of her. But I guess I would be too, especially from the little scene you two gave earlier. That's why I waited for my men to make their grand entrance."

I suddenly felt sick as I looked at Zuri. She looked pale as she sat down on the couch.

"You were watching us?"

"I do have cameras in your place, Damon. Remember, I had to watch your every move."

"Take your men and get the hell out of here. Now!"

Milo looked at me and smiled. "Just remember you and her have a job to do. I don't care how you both do it, but it needs to be done immediately. If not, I will personally see to it that you both are floating in the Carter River, along with where these two are going. Got it?"

I didn't say a word as he gently slapped my cheek before going to the door. Two men came in to grab the guys we shot before Milo smiled and walked out.

Zuri glanced at me with the same scared look she had earlier. I took her hand and took her to the room. I grabbed her bag as I got one of my own and began throwing stuff inside.

"I can't stay here, and you can't stay at Nicole and Chandler's."

"Where are we going? And what about Nicole and Chandler? Milo knows where they stay, so even if we disappear, he can still harm them."

"I know, that's why I'm going to have them and your parents go on an extended vacation. Just until all of this blows over."

"They can't just stop what they're doing and leave, Damon! They have jobs and lives here."

"I think they would rather go hide out then get killed," I said while continuing to throw clothes in my bag.

"What about us? Where are we going?"

I looked at her and sighed. "First, we have to get everyone in a safe area, somewhere that won't tip Milo off. I could ask Uncle Julian if there're some places they could go. As for their jobs, the only thing I could do is have some undercover guys watch them. I don't know how effective it'll be, but it'll be something if Milo's men try to mess with anyone."

"Do you think he would, even if we're agreeing to his demands?"

"Maybe he won't right now, but he will if we're not moving fast enough."

"But he didn't give a time limit."

"Trust me, he did. Now, I need for you to convince your parents to leave their house. You think you can do that?"

"And where are they going to go?"

"Leave that to me, okay Z?" I said. I picked up my phone and called my uncle. Hopefully he'll have something available for everyone to stay.

Zuri

I nervously wrung my hands together while staring at my parents' house. This was my first day back in the city and so much was going on that I felt I was losing it. Now I have to face my parents, which was something I was trying to avoid since arriving back. Not only that, but Damon decided to come with me, which probably wasn't the best idea considering that my parents, particularly my dad, was still hung up over what happened in L.A. If he sees me with another man, especially a white man, we might not have to worry about Milo coming after us, because my dad would kill us both.

"You know what, you don't even have to come in. I got this."

"Zuri, I'm the one providing a place for them to stay, so I think I should be present."

"And what are we going to tell them?"

"Let me handle that, okay baby?"

I stared at him while his finger lightly brushed against my cheek. He leaned me to him while I tried to control my breathing. Before he could even kiss me, we heard tapping on the window. I looked over and saw my dad by the car, looking at us with a strange look. I sighed, figuring it was time to face the music.

I opened the door and gave him a huge hug. "Hey, Dad. How is everything?"

"Taking things one day at a time. I'm glad you came by since you were in town almost the entire day."

I sighed, realizing he was going to say something about me not coming by. I was going to. I didn't think it was going to be this soon though.

"And who's this?" he asked while pointing at Damon.

"Hello, sir, I'm Damon Baxter. I'm a friend of Zuri's," he said. He extended his hand out for a handshake, but my dad didn't accept it. Typical of him.

"Why don't we go inside and talk. Is Mom here?" I asked, while quickly going to the door.

"She's in the kitchen," my dad said while still looking at Damon. He glanced at me wondering what the hell was going on as I gave him a look reading "not now".

We walked into the house, and sure enough, my mom was in the kitchen cooking dinner. I went up to her and gave her a hug.

"Oh sweetie, I didn't think you would stop by so soon. How is everything?"

"Everything is great so far. In fact, couldn't be better."

"And who is this?" my mom asked while coming up to Damon. She gently grabbed his hand and stared at him, which I could tell was making him uncomfortable.

"Mom, this is Damon Baxter. He's a friend of mine. He's also good friends with Nicole's husband, Chandler."

"Humph," my dad mumbled before going to the living room. My mom rolled her eyes and smiled at Damon.

"Well, nice to meet you, Damon. Might I add, you are one fine looking young man."

"Thanks, Mrs. Caldwell."

"Call me Daphne. You have an older brother or perhaps your dad is available. If they look anything like you, I wouldn't mind getting to know them."

"Mom!"

"Of course she would act like that. Damn hussy," my dad said while going to the refrigerator.

"Shut the hell up, Clyde. Just because you're not getting none of this, you expect no one else to."

"Hell, no one wants your dried up ass."

"Oh wow," I said while lowering my head. My parents can be a fucking embarrassment sometimes.

"Then why the hell are you steady begging for it then?"

"Trust me, I don't have to beg. If you want that over there, go have it. You practically bang everyone in the damn neighborhood anyway."

Damon came up to me as he tried to hold back from laughing. "Are they always like this? And should I get them single places to stay in?"

"Yes and no. And stop laughing," I said while shoving him. He put me in his arms and whispered.

"Now I see where you get your feistiness from."

"Well, that part I'm proud of."

"Among other things. Hopefully I'll get to see that side of you again."

I smiled and he sucked on my earlobe. For him to do be doing that in front of my parents had my pussy wet. Being around him is a damn challenge. I can get horny at the wrong place at the wrong time.

"What are you two doing over there?" my dad asked.

"Nothing, Dad. Now, can we please get back to the topic at hand, which is me being here."

"And your guest."

"Yes. Can we all just please sit down so we can talk."

"I'd rather stand. Are you going to announce that you two are together? Didn't you just break up with Tyrik not too long ago?"

"That was a mistake that I'm still living with. As for Damon, we've known each other for a long time and we recently reconnected."

"You've just been in town for a few hours, so how have you two 'reconnected?'" my dad stressed.

"Just know that we're together, okay Dad? Anyway, there's a reason for why we're here."

"Besides that little announcement?" he asked.

"Since you two haven't been on a vacation in a while, we were hoping that you two would like to pack a few things and go off to St. Croix. Damon's uncle owns a resort there, and as a gift from me to you two, I wanted to do something special."

"What's the catch?" my mom asked.

"There's no catch. I know I put you both through some things with what happened in L.A., that's why I wanted to do this for you both. Damon was gracious enough to do this, especially since the resort is one of the most popular ones on the island."

"Why are you trying to get rid of us? Did he put you in some type of shit, Zuri?" my dad asked.

"No! Why would you think that?"

"The fact that he conveniently has a place for us to stay in. I don't trust your story as much as I don't trust him. You know how I feel about his kind."

Damon sighed and I looked at him. Now he probably knows why I never told my parents about him. Frankly because my dad disapproves of interracial dating. He kind of has his ways towards different races in general, but having me dating anyone outside of my race is a slap in the face to him.

"Do we really have to go there, Dad?"

"Yes, we do. I told you if you bring someone like him in my house, then you and him are not welcome. Hell, I'm surprised I even let you in the door."

"Stop it, Clyde!" my mom yelled.

"No, in fact, I'm not going anywhere that you two suddenly planned. For all I know, you two probably planning on doing something to us."

"Dad, will you get that silly mess out of your head. I just wanted to do something nice for you, that's all. No strings attached."

"Can I say something, Mr. Caldwell?"

"I don't want your opinion."

"That's enough! Zuri, we will take your offer up and go. Hell, I would love to go to St. Croix, so I'm all for it. How long is the stay?"

"Two weeks."

"Yeah, you're trying to get rid of us," my dad said. He came over to Damon and gave him a heated look. Before he could even say anything, my mom pulled him away from Damon and took him to their bedroom.

Once they closed the door, Damon shook his head. "I'm sure your dad is a joy to be around at family events."

"That's how he is. What you see is what you get."

"I'm sure. Now I see why you never introduced me to him. I just thought it was because I was your professor."

"That's something else he would never know."

"Baby, despite how your dad is, I'll still help him. He's important to you, so of course I'll do what I can to keep him safe."

I smiled. "Thank you."

He nodded. "Okay, so they'll go to St. Croix and I already spoke with Chandler. Since him and Nicole will go visit his family in Boston, we don't have to worry about a hideaway for them. But just in case, I'll give him tickets to go to St. Croix as well."

"And how are you going to keep Milo off of their trail?"

"Simple, they'll all have aliases, so no one would bother to look for the names I created."

"But wouldn't they know that everyone is gone?"

He smiled. "You need to stop worrying so much. My uncle and I have everything under control."

"Fine, but what about us? And your job? You can't just stop teaching."

"I can if I said I have to take care of my uncle for two weeks. As for a place, he gave us somewhere we can go. That is, if you can handle being with me day in and day out, in the same room, watching me getting undressed, taking showers…"

"You're full of it."

"And you'll probably be touching yourself, which I wouldn't mind seeing, but only if I can finish you off."

He walked toward the door, turned around, and flashed that smile of his before going outside. I had to fan myself, thinking about that moment. Ugh I hate him.

He walked back inside with the tickets for my parents' trip. He handed them to me before putting me in his arms and giving me a passionate kiss. He kissed my neck before going down to the dip between my breasts. His tongue slowly went across my chest, which had me moaning. Hopefully my parents didn't hear that.

The door opened and my parents came back in the living room. My mom smiled while my dad looked pissed.

"When will we be leaving?" she asked.

"Now. I was able to get you two first class tickets. Your plane will be leaving in two hours from Hobby, so I suggest you pack what you can and head on out."

"I still want to know what you're up to. This shit doesn't seem right at all," my dad chided.

"I assure you Mr. Caldwell that all of this is legit and it's just a good gesture from your daughter's heart. Now, do you have anything packed?"

"Of course I do. I'll pack some things for you Clyde."

"I can pack my own shit."

"Well, you should go and do it," Damon said.

My dad pointed his finger at him and surprisingly, Damon didn't budge. The two went into the room and closed the door.

"He better be glad I didn't break that damn finger."

"Damon."

"I'm trying to be nice and cordial, but your dad is being an ass. I get it, he doesn't want you dating a white man, but does he have to keep saying something stupid every five seconds."

"That's just how my dad is. He gave Tyrik a hard time too and he's black."

"That I can understand."

I took his hand and we walked outside. Damon gave a confused look as I unlocked his car door and got in the back seat. I motioned for him to come as he stared at me, not sure what to do.

"In your parents' driveway? Are you crazy?"

"Damon Baxter is scared? Wow, that's a first."

"Your dad might come out here with a damn shotgun."

"You have dangerous men and a crime boss after you and you're worried about my dad?"

Damon smiled. "Because he's your dad, Z. Every man has that thought when it's with the woman they're with."

I blushed. "Come here."

He got in the backseat and closed the door. I found a sun shield visor in the back and put it up as he smiled.

"I was wondering where that was."

I pulled down his pants while he did the same for me. I turned my back to him and sat on his lap, which was a little uncomfortable, and slowly slid him in me. I shuddered at the feel of him as he put his hands underneath my shirt, feeling my breasts, making the sensation even more thrilling.

I started riding him, hoping we didn't get caught, but I was horny and I couldn't wait until we left to be with him.

"You couldn't wait until we got to our spot?" he whispered.

I didn't want him to talk, so I leaned my body back, rolling my hips unto him, which had him moaning. That was the only thing I wanted to hear.

My first climax went through me as he grabbed my hips and slammed me down on him, giving me a sensitive sensation, but it felt so good. He did it again, which had me gripping the back of the passenger seat.

"Cum all over me, baby."

My legs started shaking as our bodies were in sync with each other. I couldn't stop the scream that came from me as my body started to shut down. I leaned my head back on his shoulder as his orgasm went through me. I started to become a little worried about being with him without a condom, which was an issue I had when we first started dating. I knew I shouldn't be worried now after the deed was done, or worried about the fact that we could have been watched by Milo, but I guess that's not a factor now.

"Gets better every time we're together," Damon whispered.

"Yes, it does, but we better get ourselves together before my parents start looking for us."

While we did our best to clean up, we were able to pull ourselves together and go back inside. My parents were sitting on the couch with looks on their faces, wondering where we were. My mom started to laugh while my dad looked at her and rolled his eyes.

"Are you ready? We can drive you to the airport?" I asked.

"I think we should take my car. You never know what you'll find in yours," she said to Damon. He looked at me, trying not to laugh. I guess my dad was the only one who didn't get it, which I'm glad he didn't.

"Okay, we need to head out," Damon said while grabbing my mom's suitcase. She smiled, telling him how much of a gentleman he was, which pissed my dad off even more.

"You wouldn't have done it," she said to him.

"Damn right."

I shook my head and looked at Damon. He gave me a wink before going out to the door. I don't know what's going to happen between us, but I hope it works for us this time around. I just hope I stick around long enough for it to.

Damon

After dropping Zuri's parents off at the airport, the two of us headed to my uncle's cabin to get ourselves situated. His place was in the middle of nowhere, so it would be good for us, and Milo wouldn't be on our trail.

Zuri put her bags down on the chair and looked around.

"This is nice."

"Yeah, my unc knows how to put things into place."

"Will you be returning my mom's car?"

"Nope. It would be best if we switched off cars anyway, so no one would be suspicious."

She nodded. "That's fine. So will Julian be coming by?"

"Probably, but now, we need to find out about Tyrik's whereabouts. Do you know if he makes trips to the city, or just stays in L.A.?"

She sighed. "I wouldn't know his whereabouts. I said before we haven't talked since I was forced out of Randall."

"Do you know if anyone would know where he's at? Do you still associate with anyone from Randall?"

"I can probably call Erin. I still talk to her every now and then."

"Cool. Call her up and see where he'll be in the next two weeks. Wherever he is, then that's where we'll be."

She nodded and pulled out her phone. I took a burner phone from the cabinet near the TV and handed it to her.

"Don't use your phone, it might be tapped."

"How in the hell would it be? And how will I contact anyone?"

"There're plenty of phones here. I know enough about this place to know where everything is placed."

"But how do we know it's tapped?"

"With Milo, anything is possible. Now, call."

She sighed and went through her phone to get her former co-worker's number. While she was on the phone, someone was knocking at the door, which had me a little startled. Once the person started doing a special knock, I knew who it was. I opened it, giving my uncle a hug.

"Hey unc."

"Hey D. I see you got yourself into some shit."

I sighed. "It wasn't me this time."

"Don't blame the pretty lady for this. I told you not to mess with Milo the first time around. Just because you stop taking orders from him, doesn't mean you got out of the business. You'll always be in for life."

He looked at Zuri and smiled. "Hey sweetie," he said, giving her a hug.

"Hi Julian. I wish we were meeting under better circumstances."

"Me too, but regardless, it's good to see you."

"Likewise."

"Did you find out where Tyrik is?" I asked.

"Yep. He'll be in L.A. for a month. In fact, Randall is hosting a party for Malcolm next week."

I nodded. “Okay. Well, I guess we’re going to L.A. then. You think you can handle going back there?”

“Honestly, no, but I just want this done.”

“Same here.”

“D, if you need help, then I’m available,” my uncle suggested.

“You have been more than helpful, Unc. Thank you for doing what you did for everyone.”

“Of course. I know how Milo can be, so you need to do what you can to get him off your back.”

“Did you know Milo before Damon got involved with him?” Zuri asked.

Julian looked at me and I rubbed the back of my neck. That was something else Zuri didn’t know.

“I guess Damon never told you. Did you want me to say anything?” he asked while staring at me.

I shrugged and went to sit down. Julian sighed and stared at Zuri.

“Damon’s parents worked for Milo. They were killed during one of their assignments.”

Zuri looked shocked while I put my head in my hands. I took several deep breaths, not wanting to go into details, but I knew Zuri would ask.

“You said they were killed in a car accident.”

“That part was true. They were killed then, but it was during a job that Milo asked them to do. They were after some guy, Escobar

Mendoza. He was a guy that Milo wanted out of his territory. While Damon's mom, Teresa, was trying to distract the guy, my brother Paul was trying to find his mark to shoot him. Something or someone must have tipped the guy off, because a couple of men started firing at the two. They shot as many as they could, but they were outnumbered, so to protect themselves, they got into a SUV to get away from them.

"Unfortunately, the SUV lost control and fell off a bridge. It hit a couple of boulders before landing in the water. Teresa was already killed, but Paul held on for a couple of days before dying in the hospital. The injuries were too much to bare."

"And Paul told you everything?" Zuri asked.

"Yeah, before he passed. He believed the accident was deliberate."

"Why would he think that?"

Julian looked at me and took another deep breath.

"Because my mom was cheating on my dad with Milo," I softly said.

Zuri gave a wide-eyed look as she sat down beside me. "Wow."

"Paul never let on that he knew about Teresa and Milo, so he continued on with his missions, thinking that things could change or someone would finally fess up."

"But this still doesn't make sense. Who would set up the two if Milo didn't know that your dad knew about the affair?" Zuri asked.

"Milo wasn't no dummy. He knew that Paul had his suspicions. He also knew that Paul was going to do something about it, but didn't know when and where. That's why he took it upon himself to eliminate my brother before he could do it to him," Julian answered.

"Wow, that's crazy."

"Anyway, we think that Milo tipped off Escobar, making my parents become off guard to what was happening," I said.

"So you decided to get involved with Milo to find out if your parents were murdered," Zuri said.

"I needed to know the truth. I knew Milo was bad news and I didn't want my parents' deaths to be forgotten. That's why I joined Milo's organization. Unfortunately, I wasn't able to find anything. That's why I got out."

"Technically, I asked for you to get out. I never liked the idea of you doing this," Julian said.

"Someone had to. You sure didn't."

"Because I didn't want to be caught up in something I couldn't get out of. Just like you almost did. Instead of you finding out anything, you were doing his dirty work and killing people."

"Which is something I'm not proud of, but I had to be convincing, so that's why I had to do what was necessary to find out the truth."

"Even killing people?" Zuri asked.

"Some of them did kind of pissed me off."

"Wow," she said and got up.

"Zuri, please don't look at me any differently. We were getting back into a good place. Besides, even if I didn't get involved with Milo, he would have found some way to mess with me because I was Teresa and Paul's son. He wanted to recruit me, so when I finally agreed, he was more than willing to do it. Do you remember those guys from the diner when we first met?"

Zuri thought about it before speaking. "Yeah, I think so. Why?"

"They were Milo's men. There was a job I had to do earlier that night, which I did. They were there to see if anything else was going to go down."

"That's why you wanted to go there. So, if anything did, I would have been in the crossfire."

"I wouldn't have let that happen."

"But you wouldn't have known, Damon! It seems as if every time I let my guard down with you, I keep learning more crazy things about you! Is there anything else you have buried that you want to expose? Please tell me now while everything is in the open."

"I don't have anything else to hide. Unlike you, who still hasn't told me what you've been hiding from five years ago."

We stared at each other when Julian cleared his throat.

"I don't mean to get into your business, but although what Damon did was wrong, he was trying to find out what really happened with his parents and that was the only way to go," Julian said.

Zuri sighed. "I get that, but it's the fact that you withheld information from me again."

"I realize that, but like I said, I wanted to protect you, Zuri."

She nodded. "I guess that's something I have to realize. But besides him being your uncle, how does Julian play into this?

"Because I was working on the other side of the law. I'm a retired police officer."

Zuri smiled. "I guess you never imagine having family on the other side?"

"Nope, but I still love them and I'll help them anyway I can."

I went over to Zuri who was looking into my eyes. I put her hand into mine and gave her a pleading look.

"Are you mad at me?"

She sighed. "I should be, but I'm not. I just wish you were straightforward with me."

"I understand that, but I need the same in return."

Zuri nodded and Julian cleared his throat again.

"Before I head out, I need to know, is everything cool?"

"It is, Unc. Thanks."

"And you both have a plan?"

"Yep. We just need to get some tickets to L.A."

"Leave that to me," he said.

I patted him on the back as he was about to leave. He hugged Zuri before going to the door.

"Wow. I didn't know so much was going on."

"I'm sorry I didn't tell you at first, but I didn't want to give away too much information on the first night. But when I saw you again, I wanted to get to know you. That's why I kept it to myself. I figured you wouldn't understand anyway."

"Surprisingly, I do. You want to avenge your parents' death. But what if it was just hearsay and it was just an accident?"

"If so, then it was, but I know Milo. I don't know how he did it, but it happened. Now that we're in this mess, I'm going to continue digging until I find the proof that I need."

"Let me help you."

I shook my head. “You already have enough going on.”

“Damon, I want Milo to get what he deserves, so if there’s anything I can do, then I want to do it.”

I smiled. “I know I won’t be able to stop you, huh?”

She shook her head. “Nope, so you might as well let me into your plan.”

“Okay, but if anything crazy is about to happen, I’m pulling you out.”

“Damon, there’s no point to if Milo wants me involved. Whether you like it or not, I’m going to be a part of it.”

“Fine, but get your things together, because once Julian comes back with the tickets, we’re leaving.”

Zuri nodded and I kissed her.

“Are you ready to go on this ride with me? I should warn you though, it will get a little messy.”

Zuri smiled. “Ready as I’ll ever be.”

She sat down and I went to the window, looking at how beautiful the day looked. Too bad we can’t enjoy it. Hopefully once everything blows over, Zuri and I can have those moments together.

Zuri

I stared out the airplane window, becoming nervous to be going to L.A. I just left there, so I didn't want to go back and face the humiliation that I experienced. I glanced over at Damon who was listening to music on his phone. He looked over at me and kissed the side of my neck.

"I know you're nervous, but don't be. It'll be okay."

"That's kind of hard not to be when I have to face the same people that belittled me."

"This time, I'll be there, so there's no need to worry. I have an idea to loosen you up."

"I wonder what that is."

"If you meet me in the restroom, then I can show you."

"I'm not joining the Mile High Club with you, Damon."

"Wow, Zuri Caldwell is scared. That's the first."

I glanced at him and playfully rolled my eyes. "Surprisingly, I'm not in the mood."

"Oh really, maybe I can change your mind," he said as he gently nibbled on my ear while rubbing on my thigh. Wow, we have only seen each other for a couple of hours and we have pretty much fucked the entire day. Not sure how that's possible since we were dodging bullets and my parents throughout the day, but I guess that brings out the horny side for the both of us.

"Come on, you know you want to," Damon whispered as his hand was going to my center. He grabbed my blanket, which was nearby, and draped it over my legs. He kissed my neck and whispered, “If we don’t go in there, then I’ll make you cum right here.”

“And we’re going to get kicked off this plane.”

“It’ll be so worth it.”

“Can you ever turn the horniness off?”

“Not when I’m around you.”

I blushed and he smiled. “Okay, you’re right. We should be focusing on what we have to do and not trying to get each other off. So, why don’t we do something else, like look through Tyrik’s profile?”

“I pretty much know who Tyrik is, so I don’t need to look through his profile. But I need to know, where are we staying?”

“Already have a room booked at the Omni L.A. under the name Wesley and Amanda Preston.”

“Nice.”

“Now, have you changed your mind about joining me in the restroom?”

I smiled and laid a hand on his chest. “No, but maybe you can make me feel good right here.”

He smiled as I laid my head on his shoulder. “Just know that whatever we’re going through, we’re in it together, okay?”

I nodded as I felt his hand rub between my thighs. I leaned back, enjoying the flight and the sensation from him as I started to relax, which was something I haven’t done in a while.

***

Once our flight was over and we got our bags, we were at our room at the Omni getting ready to meet up with Erin and her husband, Roger. Erin were preparing for Malcolm's party coming up and she needed a hand getting everything started. Hopefully my former boss, Randall, doesn't realize I'm helping because he'll probably have my ass arrested since I'm banned from the company.

Since our outing will consist of dinner and going to a club, we had to dress up since where we were going was pretty swanky. I watched Damon as he was putting on a blue dress shirt that matched his eyes. I've never seen him dressed in anything but jeans, a T-shirt, and sometimes a sweater for class, so it was kind of odd seeing him semi-dressed. I liked what I saw, which made me a little horny. I really need to control myself.

He looked and smiled. "Look at you, and you say I need to turn off my horniness."

"Stop. It's just a surprise to see you like this, that's all."

"I have to admit, you do look sexy. So sexy that I don't even want to leave."

He came over to me and put his arms around my waist. I gave him a seductive smile before pulling away from him and going to the dresser. He gave a sexy sigh. The round neck half sleeve white dress was perfect for the evening. I've been to the club we're going to, so I knew I had to step up my game, and possibly give Damon something to think about during our night out.

He came over to me and kissed my exposed back, as he grinded my ass onto him. His lips went lower as I moaned. I'm trying not to give into him, but it was hard not to.

"You know I'll go lower," he whispered.

Before I could say anything more, he pulled up my dress and put his arm around my waist. He led me over to the bed and stripped off my clothes. I did the same for him as he turned me around and leaned my body against him. His hand was caressing me while his lips were kissing my shoulder as a thrilling sensation came over me. He bent me over while still holding me as I slowly felt him go in me. His lips were going down my back as we moved in a steady pace, feeling every inch of him going in me. I tilted my head back, enjoying the feel as he grabbed my hair.

"Fuck, yes," I whispered. He knew I like that, which made the moment even sexier.

His lips were sucking my skin as he was finding his rhythm. The sounds of our bodies moving together were the only sounds in the room, which made me even more excited. I couldn't hold in my orgasm as I gripped the sheets, pulling them as the first wave hit. I already knew that I would have more coming, which I didn't mind at all.

He pulled out, which had me a little disappointed, but it wasn't to stop, it was to switch positions. He smiled as he laid me down and took both of my hands into his.

He stared into my eyes as we started our journey again, this time, a little more passionate and intimate. Although I love all types of positions with him, this is the one that I loved the most. It connected us and made us one. That's the most gratifying feeling anyone could ever have when they're making love, and even though we never said those words to each other, I think we both knew we were in that moment in our lives.

I pulled him closer to me, my hands going down his back while he looked into my eyes. My heart was racing as he closed his eyes, enjoying me as much as I was enjoying him. That was a feeling that I never wanted taken away from us.

***

I laid in bed with a smile on my face. After our session, I didn't even want to leave the room, but I knew we had to since we were meeting Erin and Roger soon. She texted me letting me know they were running late anyway, so it gave us some time to freshen up and get ready again.

After taking another shower, I put my dress back on while Damon was putting on his shirt again. He looked over at me and smiled. “You know you’re still going to have to keep me off of you tonight.”

"Oh really? You still haven’t had enough of me?”

“I could never have enough of you. You know that.”

I blushed and looked in the mirror. “I’m kind of nervous about seeing Erin.”

“Why?”

“I guess I’m still feeling some type of way with how everything went down. Also, it’s kind of odd that she would want my help on an event. She has my job now, so she should be able to know what to do and what type of ideas to have.”

“Consider it a good thing since that’s your ticket for being around Tyrik.”

“That’s true. I have kind of snooped online and saw a party that she organized before I returned to Houston. It was a disaster.”

“See, now everyone will know you were the mastermind behind throwing the best parties.”

I nodded. “Maybe so.”

I still was feeling a bit uneasy about everything. I wondered if it was a good idea to go through with this plan.

Damon continued to get ready as he grabbed his .45, which had me a bit panicky.

“D, you know you can’t have your gun out.”

"I'm only going to have it in the car. Even though it's not going to help me if anything does happen."

"You mean if someone is following us or if you see Tyrik?"

Damon sighed. "That I haven't decided on."

I grabbed my clutch as Damon continued to look at me. "I have to ask, how did you pack up anything that fast, especially that outfit you have on. Hell, I might have to have my gun in case I have to put a bullet in someone's ass for looking at you."

I laughed. "Damon, no one is going to hit on me, especially if you're around."

"You'll be surprise, sweetheart. Besides, why wouldn't they? Look at you."

"If you must know, since I didn't have time to unpack, I still had majority of my party clothes in my suitcase. I knew the scene here, so of course I had to dress the part."

"Okay, well we better head out."

I went up to Damon and looked into his eyes. "Promise me that nothing will happen tonight."

"Why would you think it would?"

"Because Tyrik might be there. That's the club he frequents. That was also the place where he proposed to me at."

Damon gave me a strange look and sighed. I probably should have told him that beforehand.

"Wait, so who thought of going there?"

"Roger did."

"You don't think I won't say anything to Tyrik if I see him? You're delusional if you think that."

"Damon, please. We have to get a feel of him and what his plans might be before we do anything. For all we know, he might know what's going on and have a plan of his own. You should know that you can't go somewhere without thinking rationally about what your game plan is."

"Yes, I do know, and if I see him, then I won't do anything. However, if he comes at me wrong, then that's a different story."

"D, if you see him, please don't act crazy."

"Baby, we were going to see him eventually. Just because we might tonight does not mean I'll start shooting at him. Like you said, we need to have a game plan and figure out what we should do that doesn't involve killing him, but possibly exposing Milo."

"Seriously?"

"Yes. Besides being with you, Tyrik hasn't done anything to me, so I don't have a reason to want to kill him. Maybe rough him up a little, but not kill him."

"I just don't want anything crazy to happen."

"And it won't, trust me."

I gave him a doubtful look and he laughed. "Seriously, Zuri. You don't trust me?"

"I do, but…"

"Baby, out of respect to you, nothing will happen, okay?"

I nodded. "Okay."

"Alright, now we better go."

I nodded, taking several deep breaths, hoping that this night doesn't turn into a bloodbath.

Damon

Once we left our room, Zuri gave me directions on where to go, which was a restaurant and nightclub rolled into one. I checked myself in the visor mirror and Zuri laughed. I looked at her, wondering what was so funny.

"I can't look at myself?"

"I've never seen you check yourself out, that's all. You usually never cared about how you looked."

"Well, there's a first for everything. Do you know if they're here yet?"

She looked at her phone and nodded. "They're here."

"Okay, let's get this show started."

I found the nearest parking spot and we got out. As soon as we approached the building, Zuri immediately saw her friend and went up to her for a hug.

"Erin!"

"Hey, Z!"

As the two got reacquainted, I looked over at Roger who gave a nod. I did the same, not knowing what else to do. I'll let Z have her time with her friend. From what I know, Erin was the only friend she had left after everything went down, so at least she stuck by her and didn't judge her like everyone else did.

"Erin, I would like for you to meet a very good friend of mine, Damon. Damon, this is Erin."

"So, this is the infamous Damon. It's very nice to meet you," Erin said while giving me the stare. I know that stare from anywhere, which was a little crazy considering her husband was standing nearby.

"Nice to meet you," I said.

"Zuri has told me a lot about you. Now I see why you were so hung up on him, Z."

"Yeah, we're back together now," I said.

"Oh really? That's too bad. Damn, that's really too bad."

She continued to look at me while I looked at Zuri who was ready to claw her eyes out. She looked over at Zuri and smiled.

"I didn't mean anything by it, Z. You know Roger and I are swingers, so of course if I see an attractive man, I'm going to want to talk to him."

"That's fine, as long as it's not my man. Do it again and you won't like what I'll do to you."

"Is that threat?"

"It's a promise. Now, shall we start our evening?" she said as she took my hand and went to the door. I glanced at her and saw she was heated, which to me was a damn turn on.

"Don't even start, Damon."

"I wasn't going to say anything except that you held your own. But I have to say, if that's your friend, then I hate to see who your enemies are."

"Trust me, those are not a factor."

"If you want to end this, then we can. We can probably find another way to track down Tyrik."

"No, we're going to use Erin. Even if you have to come on to her since she wants to fuck you."

I gave her a strange look and she laughed. "I'm kidding. I wouldn't do you like that. I would have to kill her before I let her be with you."

"You do know you're turning me on right now."

"I'm sure I am. Get your mind out of the gutter and do what we came here to do, shall we?"

"Of course."

We went to a table that Erin already reserved as she gave us an apologetic look. "I'm really sorry you two. I was already drinking when we got here, so of course, I'm drunk. So whatever I just said was due to the alcohol."

"Yep, blame it on the alcohol," Roger mumbled.

Erin gave him the evil eye before looking at us again. "So, again, I'm sorry. Anyway, it's good to see you, Z. You look beautiful as always."

"Thanks. I can't say the same about you," Zuri said and smiled.

Erin looked hurt while Roger chuckled.

"Anyway, what are you doing in L.A.? I thought you were leaving for good."

"Change of plans. I decided to come back because I realized no matter what happened, this is my home. Well, that, and because Damon and I wanted to start fresh."

"In the city that you were humiliated in?"

"It wasn't the city. It was me and my actions that got me booted from my career."

"Don't you feel bad about what happened? Evidently you don't with Tyrik since you're with Damon now."

"Tyrik is the one who broke up with me, so why should I wallow in self-pity?"

"I don't know. I mean, Tyrik is one of the people that can make or break your career. Say if he does see you with Damon, he could blacklist you from going with another company."

"I'm not worried about Tyrik. Besides, I'm sure I can find another company, I just haven't had the time to."

"Despite your little hiccup, I'm glad that you're back and willing to help me. I miss you at Randall."

"I do too, but that's life, right?"

I looked over to the entrance when I saw someone looking at our table. I already knew who it was, so I was ready for whatever was about to go down.

"Look who's here," Erin whispered to Zuri as he made his way to the table. I could tell she was getting nervous as she looked at me. I looked ahead, saying nothing, since I didn't want to start anything.

"Hey, Zuri."

"Tyrik."

He said hi to Erin and Roger before looking at me. "I'm not sure if I know you."

"You wouldn't know me."

"He's my man, Tyrik," Zuri said.

He smiled, giving a small chuckle, which was pissing me off.

"What the hell is so funny?" I asked.

"Nothing, just that Zuri moved pretty fast. We just broke up not too long ago and you're already with someone. I should have known what you were all about anyway."

Zuri jumped up and Erin and I tried to calm her down, but I already knew that was impossible.

"What does that supposed to mean? You broke up with me after what happened. It was your idea to get me stupid drunk since you figured it was your dad's party and you wanted me to have fun. For all I know, you probably set me up."

"I wouldn't have a reason to do that, Zuri. Despite what you think, I care about you. Hell, I still do."

"You have a funny way of showing it. But you don't have to worry about me. I'm doing just fine."

"With him?"

"Yes, with him. So why don't you go live your life and leave me the hell alone. You didn't care about me anyway, so we'll keep it that way."

"That's fine, go live your life with him. Don't expect to come back to me when you're bored with him."

"Trust me, I'll never be bored with Damon."

"I'm sure. Fucking slut."

I jumped past Zuri and Erin and got in Tyrik's face. I knew he was going to start something, so I was ready for it.

"You're a real bitch to say that to her when you're the one who ruined her life and career."

"Please, she'll tell you anything to play like she's the victim."

"I know your type. You hide bchind your daddy's money and figured you can do whatever you want. You're a coward and you did her a favor by leaving her."

"She already got you pussy whipped, but I can see why. She definitely got some good pussy."

I grabbed him by his shirt as Roger tried to pull me off of him. One of Tyrik's friends tried to do the same to him as I punched him across his jaw.

"Keep talking like that and I'll kill your ass!"

"You don't know what I'm capable of, muthafucker. Come after me again and you'll be the one dealt with!"

I pushed past Roger and I used my fist to shut Tyrik up. Zuri tried to push me off of him, causing the two of us to fall on the restaurant floor.

Security finally came over to us as they pulled me up, and Tyrik as well.

"Show is over you two. You're both leaving."

"Do you know who I am?" Tyrik yelled.

"We know who you are, Tyrik O'Neal, and we're tired of your mess. Cause another disturbance and we'll have you banned from here," one of the security said as they took him outside. A second later, I was thrown out too as Zuri came over to me.

"Are you okay? I didn't want that to happen, but I knew it would," she said while touching my bloody lip.

"I'm fine, Zuri. He just got in my face and I lost it, especially when he was talking about you."

"I'm sorry."

"Why are you apologizing? He's the asshole. Just for that, I don't think you should be talking to him."

"But I have to because of Milo."

"I don't want you around him. You brought up a good point about the party. Knowing him and who his father is, you might be on to something."

"Wait, you really think he could have set me up? But why?"

"That's something we have to figure out," I whispered. I could feel someone coming near us, so I didn't want to talk any further. I looked behind me and saw Erin and Roger coming to us. For some reason, I didn't trust Erin either, especially since she made that comment towards me. If she's like that in Zuri's face, then I'm sure she has done a lot of backstabbing towards people. I knew Z also felt the same way, but she wanted to keep her close to get information out of her regarding Tyrik.

"Is everyone okay?" Erin asked.

"Yeah, we're fine."

"That was intense in there, but Tyrik always had a mouth on him. Well, since we can't continue our evening, is there something else you all want to do?"

"I think we're going to call it a night, Erin," Zuri said.

"That's fine, but let me know when you want to meet up to hear my ideas regarding the party."

She nodded. "Sure, Erin. Sorry tonight didn't go as planned."

She smiled. "It's okay. It was really nice to meet you, Damon. And again, sorry about earlier."

"No problem. Have a good night."

Roger said the same as the two went over to their car. I looked at Zuri and smiled.

"You really not going to let a punk ass ruin our night, are you?"

She shook her head. "Not at all. I just told her that so we could be alone."

"Oh really, and what did you have in mind?"

"Besides cleaning you up, I was going to take you to a couple of places that I used to frequent. We might as well make this trip fun too."

"You sure you want to do that?"

"Why not? Besides, you could be right about that night. I was so drunk out of my mind to truly remember what happened. But if I try to remember something, then it could help us and possibly expose him without having to result to killing him."

"Maybe, but we also have to figure out a way to get Milo off our backs."

"And we will. I know we don't have a lot of time, but we'll get it done."

I nodded. "So, where did you want to take me?"

She smiled and took my hand and led me to the car. This should be an interesting night.

Zuri

After going to our hotel room and getting Damon cleaned up, I took him out on the town to show him some of the places I used to go to in the city. I pulled up to 90 West Lounge, which is a lounge near the Sunset Strip. Damon looked at me while I stared ahead.

"You sure you want to go out? We didn't have to."

"I want to. It'll be fun."

We got out of the car and went to wait in line. There were a couple of people that I knew from my days at Randall that immediately spotted me and started gossiping. That would be expected, especially since this was one of the most popular spots on the strip.

We walked in and immediately grabbed a seat. I stared at Damon, wondering what he was thinking.

"What's going through that head of yours?"

He smiled. "You feel like doing something crazy?"

I gave him a worried look, wondering what he was planning. "I hate to see what that is."

"You see those guys over there?"

I tried to turn my head, but he told me not to.

"Don't look. I'm not sure if they're paparazzi or someone that Tyrik or Milo hired, but they have been following us since we left the hotel. Now my guess is that they're going to do something to us, so to make things a little easier for everyone, we're going to beat them at their own game."

"What do you have in mind?"

"Ever ran a con?"

I stared at him as he got up and pointed to the pool table.

"Does it look like I have?"

"There are a lot of things I didn't know you did, so that's possible if you have."

"No, I haven't. I wouldn't know what to do."

"It's just like getting something from your parents, or even from a man. You do a lot of lying, kissing ass, and a little begging, but you do it all for a reason and for the other person not to know what you're up to."

"I learn something new about you every hour."

"What can I say, I'm a diverse person."

"That you are. I'm guessing pool hustle?"

"You read my mind. Let's do it."

He walked towards the two guys near the end of the bar. Sure enough, they were staring at us. Damon glanced at them, giving them a slight nod.

"Enjoying the night?"

"We are, what is it to you?" one of the guys asked.

Damon smiled. "Don't worry, I'm not trying to jump either of you, if that's what you're thinking."

"Who said that we were thinking that?" the other guy asked, getting up and going to Damon.

"Whoa, relax man. I'm not trying to cause any shit tonight. I just want to have some fun with my girl and she wanted to play some pool. That's why we're here."

"You two can play by yourselves," the other guy said while drinking his beer.

"We can, but it wouldn't be interesting if we betted against each other. Let's start off with introductions. I'm Damien, and this is my girl, Zaria," Damon said while extending out his hand. One of the guys pushed it away.

"Okay, how about we make it even sweeter. How about playing for a thousand," Damon said.

The guy looked at his friend, then back at Damon. "Why choose us? There are other people here you can play against."

"We can, but we think you two will be more fun," I said while flashing a sexy smile. I glanced at Damon, who nodded.

"You better not be running any games on us."

"Do you think we would?" Damon asked.

They got up and introduced themselves as Dexter and Oliver as they followed us to the nearest table. Dexter mumbled that this would be good while Oliver was staring at me with a wicked grin. I took a deep breath, wondering what Damon's true agenda behind this. I guess I'll find out and see.

He racked up the balls while I glanced at the guys. They were deep in thought, probably trying to set up a plan.

"We'll let you break first," Damon offered.

They looked at us and Dexter shook his head. "Nah, ladies first."

I nodded and grabbed my stick and went over to break. I pushed my ass out, trying to give Damon a show, but I think I was getting someone else's attention.

"Check out my girl again and I'll push that stick up your ass."

"I'll kill you before you do that," Dexter said.

"We'll see about that."

I got the game going as I hit my ball to the left pocket. One thing that Damon didn't know was that I'm a master at pool. My dad taught me everything that I knew about the game.

Damon watched me with pride as I continued my game, hitting everything including the 8-ball. Oliver and Dexter looked at me, ready to throw down their sticks in frustration.

"You set us up, bitch!"

Damon came over to them and threw Oliver's head down onto the pool table. Several people stopped what they were doing to see what was happening.

"Listen, asshole! She won fairly. That's not our problem you both suck. Now, pay up!"

"We ain't paying you shit!" Dexter yelled.

Damon still had Oliver on the table as he kicked the pool stick up, hitting Oliver in the groin. He fell down as Damon pulled him up and threw his head onto the table as well.

"Now, I'm going to say this once again. Either you pay my girl, or I will take you both out in the alley and kill you."

"What the fuck, man? Over a game!" Oliver yelled.

"No, asshole! I know you've been following us, so who do you work for? Milo, Tyrik, or Malcolm?"

"We don't know what you're talking about!" Dexter yelled.

Damon bent Dexter's hand back and I heard a snap. I think he broke his hand.

"Damon, stop!"

"I'll break the other hand if you don't tell me who the fuck you're working for."

I looked ahead and saw two men dressed in black coming towards us. Damon shoved the two down, grabbed my hand and we went to the back exit. We ran to the side of the building and got into the car. Before security could get to us, I stepped on the gas and flew out of the parking lot, almost hitting another car coming in. I looked at Damon as he looked nervous. He glanced at me and sighed.

"I'm really sorry."

"Why are you apologizing?"

"Because I got carried away. We could have been arrested."

"You were looking out for us. You did what you had to do."

"I guess that's something else you didn't know about me. I'm a mixed martial arts fighter."

"Let me guess, Julian trained you."

"Had to. Growing up, I was bullied a lot, so he taught me a couple of things. but not a lot so I wouldn't kill anyone; just hurt them."

I looked ahead at the road, not sure what to think.

"You're not scared of me, are you?"

"Did I say I was?"

"You don't have to say anything. Your eyes are saying it all."

"It's just that I feel as if you spring something new on me every minute. First, you're an instructor, then a hitman, then a con man and now a martial arts fighter. What's next, a freaking undercover agent! You probably are and using this as a way for me to talk about Tyrik."

"Zuri, stop. You know I'm not."

"I don't know. Julian used to be a cop, so he could have easily got you into the academy."

I think I hit a nerve as he didn't say a word about my accusation. Instead, he tried to touch me, but I pulled away.

"You're a cop!"

"Listen, Zuri…"

"Wow. I don't know if I should be happy or pissed at you. At least it all makes sense now. I knew you couldn't be capable of killing people just to fit in with Milo, but you still did it."

"You know I didn't want to lie to you about that, but I had to keep my cover. Uncle Julian felt it was best."

"Is he still working for the department?"

He nodded. "Yeah, he is. We kept it a secret so you or anyone else wouldn't become suspicious. Not only are we trying to get both Milo and Malcolm off the streets, but I know without a doubt that he killed my parents."

"Were they cops too?"

He shook his head. "No, they were actually working for him. Uncle Julian tried to get them to leave, but they wouldn't. They loved the money and the rush too much. That rush is what got them killed."

I pulled into a parking lot of the hotel and stopped the car. I stared at him as he cleared his throat.

“Baby, I didn’t want to keep lying to you, but you have to realize I was doing it to protect you.”

“I need to know the entire truth, and you’re going to tell me. If you don’t, then whatever we’re doing is over.”

He nodded. “That’s fine. I’ll tell you everything, but you need to do the same for me. I need to know why you left me five years ago. And you better tell me the truth.”

I looked at him, not sure if I wanted to. If I did, I would definitely lose whatever we have going on. But he also lied, so he shouldn’t sit there and act all holier than thou.

“So, what do you say? It’s tell the truth time, so we should air everything out in the open. Are you willing to do that?”

I looked at him and nodded. “Yeah. We should.”

Damon

So Zuri figured it out. I'm a cop. Actually, a detective who has been undercover with this Milo case for too damn long. I didn't know how much longer I could have kept up the charade, so honestly, I was glad she figured it out. I wanted to tell her, but Uncle Julian felt it was better for me and for her to make her believe that I was a hitman. Even though that was bad enough, but at least my cover wasn't blown.

We were laying in the bed in our room staring at the ceiling, not knowing who would start first with their confession. I knew Zuri wouldn't with hers, so I might as well get the ball rolling.

"I first wanted to become a cop in high school after I saw my uncle be one. Watching him do his job made me feel motivated to do something good for myself and for my community. I wanted to make a difference in something and I figured joining the force to protect and serve was the best way to go. I learned a lot of things from him to get me ready for the force, especially with the martial arts, firing a gun at different angles, and knowing how to cover my tracks. That helped out when I first started and with the other cases that I was working on.

"When the case regarding Milo came up, I was eager to do it. I knew he was my parents' boss and my uncle kept mentioning what my dad said to him on his hospital bed before he died. He knew that Milo set him up because he wouldn't have had the evidence. Even though my uncle was dead set against it, I felt it was up to me to find out the truth. Not only for myself, but for him, and to give justice to my parents. That's why I did extra training to become skilled at being a mercenary and got recruited into Milo's camp."

"Was Milo ever suspicious that you could have been after him, especially since he knew that Julian was a cop?" Zuri asked.

"Not really. He figured I wanted to follow in my parents' footsteps, which I told him countless times. I used that story and continued on with trying to expose him."

"Was Julian the reason for you quitting?"

"Yeah. I felt I almost had him, but after the last person I killed, he felt I was getting in way too deep, so he forced me to quit, which I did. But he's right, even though I stopped working for him, I'm not out of the game. Case in point, everything that's happening now. Milo felt I would still be some use to him because of you. That's why he chose me to do the job even though he has someone else dealing with his killings."

"How does Julian feel about that?"

"He was upset, but once I told him that Milo threatened you, he felt I had to get back in, to protect you."

"Where does this leave me?"

"You're undercover, which means that you will do what I say."

"Are you being serious?"

"Yes, I am. Zuri, we're dealing with some dangerous men who could care less who gets in their way. They want to throw their power around so they could one up each other in getting to that top spot. All I ask of you is to do what you can to get the information that is needed so you can get out of this case."

"What if I don't, especially after what happened tonight."

"Tonight was a mishap, but we'll get back on track."

"So the hideaways that Julian had…"

"Were all provided by the department. Your parents are in a secluded resort, so nothing will happen to them. Nicole and Chandler are surrounded by plain clothed officers at all times, so they're okay as well."

"What about the guys at the diner? Were they really Milo's men or cops?"

"Why are you bringing that up?"

"Just curious."

"Yes, they were cops. One of them was actually my partner at the time. They were there because we all thought something was going to happen that night, but thank God, nothing did."

"I still can't believe this. So when you did the jobs for Milo, how did Julian feel about them?"

I sighed. "He wasn't happy about them. He was pissed, but I had to keep the front going. I couldn't stop what I was doing or I would have been killed."

"But were you ever reprimanded for it?"

I shook my head. "No."

"What if Milo finds out what you're doing? He could kill you."

"Yeah, he would, but that's a risk I'm willing to take. I'm not going to stop until scum like him and Malcolm are off the streets. If I have to die trying, then I will."

"Damon, I understand that you want to avenge your parents' deaths and do something good, but I really think we should end this. You're a cop. Don't you think you have enough evidence to put both of them behind bars, especially since you've been doing this for two years."

"I probably do, but it wouldn't be enough to hold them. They're smart, so they know what to do to cover their tracks. But I guess that means you're not mad at me."

Zuri sighed. "I want to be, but I can't. I do feel a little better knowing that you were undercover. I just wish you would have told me."

"I understand. Now that I exposed my secret, it's time to expose yours. So what you been hiding, Zuri Caldwell?

She looked hesitant as she got up and went to the window. I went up to her and put my hands around her.

"Baby, you don't have to be scared to tell me. We're being open and honest with each other."

She continued to look out the window and gave a deep breath. She turned around and stared at me.

"When I walked out on you, it wasn't because I was scared to be in a long-distance relationship, it was because of something that happened."

"Which was? You can tell me, Zuri."

"I was pregnant, Damon."

I stared at her, not sure what to say. I had to go back to the bed and sit down, processing the fact that there could be a child somewhere. *My child.*

"Wait, you said was. What happened?"

Zuri cleared her throat, trying not to cry. She would normally do that when she was on the verge of tears.

She stood in front of me and gently grabbed my hands. "I had a miscarriage."

I squeezed her hand and the tears fell down her cheeks. I picked her chin up so she could stare at me.

"Why didn't you tell me?"

"Because I didn't think you wanted to be a father. Damon, we had only known each other for six months. We really didn't know each other to raise a child."

"It wouldn't have mattered if I had known you for a few hours! I would have been there for you, you know that."

"I'm sorry, Damon. I was already scared of the idea of being pregnant, but when you told me you were a hitman, I bolted. I didn't want to raise a child in an environment where there would always be violence. You would had understood that."

"That's not any excuse! If you would have told me, we could have talked about it. You made a decision regarding our child on your own."

"I'm sorry."

"What happened?"

"It was all so sudden. I was having a lot of cramps, which my doctor said was normal, but I knew something was wrong, so I went to the ER and the doctor told me I was having a miscarriage. I think it had a lot to do with stress. I'm really sorry."

I sighed. "I would have been there for you."

She broke down in front of me, which was tearing me in two. I've never seen her like this, which gave me a mix of emotions. I stood up and stared at her while wiping the tears that had fallen. I took her hand and led her to the bed. We laid down together and I wrapped my arms around her, which made her cry even more.

"No matter what, I still care about you, Z. I always have and always will."

I kissed the back of her head, which calmed her down. After a few minutes of laying next to each other, we both fell into a deep sleep.

Zuri

I woke up, glancing at the bright sun, realizing it was morning. I looked behind me, seeing that Damon was still asleep. I touched the side of his face, feeling the stubble against his cheek. I didn't want to wake him, so I slowly got up and went into the bathroom. I pulled out one of the burner phones I got from Julian's cabin and dialed Nicole's number. I didn't know if I should call her, but I really needed someone to talk to.

After calling three times, she finally answered. "Hello?"

"Nicole, it's Zuri."

"Girl, I didn't know who you were calling unavailable. You know I don't answer anyone's call if it's unavailable."

"I'm using a burner phone. How's Chandler and Cole?"

"Everyone is fine. I just wish I could go back to my place. What in the hell did Damon do to have us go into hiding?"

"He's a cop, Nicole."

"What? He told you this?"

"He confirmed it after I figured it out. But he's dealing with some dangerous men that knows all of our lives, so that's why you had to leave. My parents also."

"I know your dad hated that."

"He doesn't know the entire truth. I just told him it was an all-expense paid vacation."

"Which knowing him, he still hated."

I softly chuckled. “I wish I could see you.”

“You never know, you just might. Julian called Chandler asking if we wanted to visit you guys. There’s a catch though. We have to be at separate hotels under aliases and possibly can’t go anywhere, but it’s fine because I want to see you.”

“Even Cole can come?”

“Actually, Julian’s footing the bill. Chandler’s parents too, so yeah.”

“Wow, that’s really nice of him.”

“He thinks it’s best in case anyone actually did follow us.”

“I’m really sorry. If I wasn’t involved with either Damon or Tyrik, none of this would be happening.”

“Stop, Z. This is not your fault. Even if you didn’t know the two, I would be still involved with Chandler, who is friends with Damon, so I would still be in the crossfire.”

“Maybe so. I just feel as if I didn’t come back in Damon’s life, then he wouldn’t have to go back to working with Milo. I am part of the reason he has to.”

“But he would have anyway since he’s working on a case. Stop blaming yourself for this, Z.”

I sighed and sat down on the toilet seat. I leaned down, feeling sick at what I was about to say.

“I lied to Damon.”

“About what?”

“About the baby. That I had a miscarriage.”

“Zuri! I thought you would have told him by now about that.”

"I couldn't tell him. He was so open and honest with me, but I couldn't tell him that I had an abortion. I couldn't tell him that I didn't want a child. I just couldn't do it."

"But you're going to have to. What if he finds out from someone else?"

"Like who? I know you won't."

"Didn't Erin take you to the clinic? How do you know she won't say anything?"

"Let's just hope that she doesn't."

"With how our lives are right now, any information could fall in the wrong hands. Just remember that."

"I don't know what to do. Damon was a little ticked that I didn't tell him about the pregnancy. Just imagine how he'll feel if I told him I terminated the pregnancy."

"Z, if you want to establish a long-lasting relationship with him, then you need to put everything on the table. Yes, it will be painful, but at least you'll have a clear conscience."

I got up and went to the mirror. I stared at my reflection, knowing that Nicole was right, but I couldn't do it.

"Maybe in time I'll tell him, but right now, I can't."

"You're hurting yourself, Z. He's not going to forgive you for this, but at least you would be honest with him."

I sighed. "I know, and that's what's tearing me apart right now."

I talked to Nicole for a few minutes before she had to go to take care of Cole. I ended the call and opened the door to see Damon near the bathroom. I looked shocked as he gave a surprised look of his own.

"You're up."

"Why wouldn't I be? I noticed you weren't in bed, so I was seeing if everything was okay."

I walked past him and went to the bed. "Everything's fine. Just had to use the bathroom. I can't pee?"

"I was just seeing if you were okay. You didn't need to have an attitude about it."

I glanced at him and sighed. "Sorry, Damon. I guess I'm just stressed out."

He came over to me and gave me a hug, which felt so good. I loved being in his arms.

"We both are. That's why I think we should find a way to release the tension, if you know what I mean."

I smiled. "Can you ever go a second without thinking about sex?"

"As I mentioned before, not when I'm around you," he said and kissed my neck.

I looked at him as he led me to the bed. Even though I shouldn't think about it, I believe he heard my conversation about the abortion. I would only know in time if he did.

Damon

After the eventful morning we had, I let Zuri sleep while I laid in the bed and watched TV. I flipped the channels, trying to find something to watch, which was unsuccessful. I turned it off and leaned down on the pillow when the doorbell rang. I got a little nervous, wondering who could be at our room. No one knew we were here since we were using aliases. I slowly got up, grabbing my pistol from underneath the bed and went to the door. I asked who it was, but no one answered. I was about to open it and start shooting when the person gave me that special knock. I sighed and opened the door to see my uncle on the other end.

"Don't scare me like that. What are you doing here?" I asked while letting him in.

"Wasn't trying to scare you, but I wanted to come by and see how you and Zuri survived your first night."

"It was definitely eventful. And she knows the truth."

"What? You told her?"

"Yeah, I wanted to be honest with her."

My uncle sat down and sighed. "Wow, I'm sure that took a lot out of you to do."

"It did, but I felt good about it. It even made her open up about the real reason why she left five years ago. She was pregnant."

"Wow, really?"

"She miscarried though."

"I'm sorry to hear that."

“So am I. Can you imagine me being a father?”

“I can see it. You’d be an excellent one.”

"Would I have been? I don't know anything about being a dad.”

“You think I did when I raised you? Just being there and being supportive and giving him or her the love they need is what matters. Yes, you have a difficult job, but that doesn’t change you as a person. You’re a bright, gifted young man who I’m proud of. I have always considered you my son, and I always will.”

I was speechless to what my uncle just said. He isn’t normally sentimental, so this was definitely a surprise to me.

“Thank you.”

“You’re welcome. Now, enough of the sentimental stuff and let’s get down to why I’m here. I received a call from the commish about what happened at that bar you were at last night. Turns out the two guys were in fact working for Malcolm O’Neal. After what happened to his punk of a son, he hired those two thugs to follow you and Zuri. At least you set them straight, even though you broke one of the guys’ hands to do it.”

“You know I wasn’t going to back down from that. I knew they were hired through either Milo or Malcolm. That was just my way of saying I was on to them.”

“Maybe so, but you have to be careful, especially now that Zuri knows that you’re undercover.”

“Unc, nothing is going to happen. I’m going to continue on the case and she’ll continue being a part of it. If the situation gets crazy, then I’ll make sure to get her out.”

“That’s if you can. You might get too deep into this that you forget what you’re focusing on. You did that five years ago when Zuri left, so I don’t want you to fall into that trap again.”

“I’m focused, unc. You don’t have to worry about me.”

He nodded. “Okay, I’ll take your word for it. But the minute that I see you losing focus, I’m pulling you out. I did it once, so I don’t have a problem doing it again.”

“Are you done?”

“Yeah, I am.”

“Good, but there’s something I need to show you,” I said and gave him my phone. While he was going off on being focused, I received a text from Milo asking to see me. That meant he was somewhere lurking in L.A.

“That didn’t take him long. Text him back to see when and where. Do you need to be wired this time?”

“I can, but it’s not going to do any good. I still have to follow his orders. We can’t get him without solid proof.”

“We know that, but if all goes well, we might have him sooner than we think.”

I looked over and saw that Zuri was still asleep. I grabbed my phone and key card.

"You want to grab some breakfast and talk about the case some more? Maybe Milo will respond with a time and place.”

“What if he wants you to bring Zuri?”

“If he wants to, that’s too damn bad, because I’m meeting with him alone.”

“You didn’t want to wait for Zuri?”

I looked back at the bed again and shook my head. “No, she needs her rest. Besides, there’s something I wanted to talk about alone.”

My uncle gave a curious look as I turned back around to watch her. I shook my head and turned to go to the door. Maybe I needed Milo to call so I could get my mind off of everything. Including what I heard from Zuri.

Zuri

I woke up and looked to my side to see that Damon was gone. I looked to the door, wondering where he could have gone to. The conversation I had with Nicole kept replaying in my mind as I thought about my confession. When I found out I was pregnant, I was scared to be a mother and didn't know what to do or how to raise a baby. The idea that I conceived a child with someone I met six months ago was also kind of disturbing. I wanted it to be with my husband, and not some guy that I slept with on the first night of meeting him.

Even though the procedure was quick and somewhat painful, it left a huge scar in my heart. I always thought about if our child would had been a boy or a girl or who he or she would look like. Our child would had been five years old, which was making me a bit emotional.

I slowly got out of the bed when my phone started to ring. Even though Damon told me to get rid of it, I still kept it in case I needed it. I picked it up and saw that it was Tyrik. I was about to put the phone down when I looked at the number again and sighed. If we were trying to expose his dad, then I should probably talk to him to see what he wanted and possibly get information out of him.

"Hello?"

"Hey. I'm surprised you answered."

"I wasn't going to."

"I'm glad you did."

"What do you want, Tyrik?"

"I wanted to apologize for last night. I took it way too far and for that, I'm sorry."

"Yeah, you did, but I don't expect anything less from you."

"I was mainly upset that you moved on with someone so soon. We just recently broke up."

"Let's rephrase that, shall we. You dumped me, remember?"

"Zuri, everything was happening so sudden with the video and the photos—"

"Which you had a part in doing. If you loved me like you claimed, you wouldn't have done what you did. And the fact that you treated me like shit when you saw me last night really put things to prospective on how you really felt about me."

"Like I said, it was because I saw you with him. I know he works for Milo Regatta. Why would you get involved with someone like him?"

"That's none of your concern. In fact, I'm hanging up, Tyrik."

"Please meet up with me. I really need to talk."

"There's nothing else to talk about."

"Maybe for you, but for me it is."

I looked to the window, contemplating if I wanted to meet him. This could help with the case if he gave out viable information. I sighed and stared ahead, knowing what I should do.

"Where did you want to meet?"

***

After I got myself together, I waited a few minutes to see if Damon would return, but he didn't. I tried calling him on one of the phones, but he didn't answer. I'm not sure where he could have gone since he doesn't know anyone here besides me. But when I noticed the keys to the rental sitting on the counter, I immediately knew he was with his uncle. He must have come while I was asleep. I grabbed the keys and went to the door. I took several deep breaths as I went to the car, still wondering what I'm doing. I shouldn't be meeting him, but in the back of my mind, I wanted answers to a lot of questions that I still had on my mind. If Damon ever finds out, then I'll have to explain it was for the case, which it was.

We both agreed to meet at Pitchoun!, which at one point was our spot. I don't know why I told him there because it would only bring up memories that I didn't want or need.

I looked around, noticing that the owner changed a few things from the last time I was there. It still felt surreal that I was here, especially with everything that was going on. For a spilt second, I was back in my social circle, enjoying everything that life has to offer.

I walked further when I immediately spotted Tyrik near the window booth. That was our table, which he asked the owner specifically to reserve for us. He had his head down, reading, when he suddenly looked up and saw me. He stood up and waited for me to come before greeting me.

"Thank you for meeting me."

I didn't say anything as I sat down.

"So you're giving me the cold shoulder?"

"You said you needed to talk, so talk."

"You don't want anything? Not even those almond tarts you like so much?"

"Tyrik…"

"Okay, you're getting irritated, so I'll talk. I felt bad for how I talked to you last night. You know I'm not like that."

"That sounded like you last night."

"But I wasn't with you. It was the idea that you were with someone else, which pissed me off. We just broke up and you already moved on. That didn't sit right with me."

"You broke up with me, remember?"

"Because of the scandal."

"That you caused."

"I didn't force you to do anything that you didn't want to do."

I leaned back in my seat and he looked at me. "Z, I didn't want things hanging like it did. You didn't deserve that. And the idea you're with Milo's enforcer is even more disturbing. I thought had better taste than that."

"I do now."

"Clever."

"You started it. Damon is a good man. He treats me better than you ever had."

"You know that's not true, Z. I would do anything for you."

"Maybe you did, but it was always at a price."

"He's dangerous, Z."

"His job is, not him."

"He chose the job, so he is."

"I could say the same about you then. Your father is a crime lord, which you failed to tell me."

"I'm assuming Baxter told you."

"At least someone did."

"I never told you about my dad because I wanted to protect you. You don't know what these guys are capable of."

"But you could have given me a warning, Tyrik. Now I could be fearing for my life since I was involved with you."

"You'll be doing that regardless since you're with Baxter. Milo is ruthless. Hell, he screwed my dad over so much that he had to get his men to go into his territory. Technically, Milo gave him the area as an alliance, but tried to take it back once my dad gave him what he wanted from him. Honestly, I don't blame him for trying to take Milo out. He's petty and sneaky."

"But do you really think that your dad should have formed an alliance knowing that Milo wouldn't have agreed to it?"

"What can I say about my dad? He has a big heart."

"Yeah, a big heart that would get him killed."

Tyrik smiled. "Maybe so. But that's the reason for the entire turf war between the two. I warned my dad, but he's his own man, so I can't be upset with him on that. But I have to ask, how did you get involved with Baxter? He doesn't seem like the guy that you would fall for."

"Why, because he's white?"

"That's not what I was talking about."

"Then what else were you referring to?"

"Because he's a hitman for starters. For what I know, you're more into the intellectual men, like myself."

"Technically, you're not all that stimulating, and Damon is also a college professor."

"Whatever."

I rolled my eyes and looked at the table. I stared back at him and sighed. "There's a lot of things I would still like to know, Tyrik. One minute, we were happy and the next we broke up."

"Z, a lot was going on at that time. Just know that I still feel bad about that night and if I could turn back time, then I would."

"Just because your dad was the one throwing the party doesn't mean I had a free pass to have fun. That was my job, as well as yours that was on the line. But of course, nothing happened to you. What did your dad do, threaten Randall to keep you onboard?"

"My dad didn't do anything. You were partly responsible for what happened, that was why you were punished."

I smiled and got up. "You have a funny way of looking at the bigger picture. I'm leaving."

"Zuri, stop."

"I have nothing more to say to you, Tyrik."

He came over to me and held my arms. I stared at him as he looked from the exit, then to me again.

"I can't give you a lot of information, especially since you're with Baxter. How do I know you won't go back and tell him anything?"

"What information do you have?"

"All I can say is that you shouldn't be in the middle of whatever is going on with Milo and my dad. That's why I tried to keep my distance, but it doesn't matter now. If you have the name, then you're a target anyway. Don't think that you're not either."

"I can handle myself."

"I know you can, but it doesn't matter. These guys are crazy and could care less who stands in their way. Just be careful, okay?"

He looked at me again, grabbed his wallet, threw a few bills on the table and walked past me.

"I still ordered those tarts for you. The hostess has them at the front," he mentioned before going to the door.

I watched him leave, wondering if I should be sincere with his gesture. A part of me wanted to because despite everything, I still cared about him.

Damon

Once my uncle and I finished our breakfast, I called Milo to see if he was in town and whether I should meet him. Sure enough, he was and wanted to meet at Grand Park near downtown. My uncle wanted to stay close by in case anything happened, but I told him I'd be fine. It wasn't the first time I was alone with him and his thugs, so this time shouldn't be any different.

I called Zuri to see if she was awake, but I didn't get an answer. Maybe she was more tired than I thought, so I'll try back later.

I borrowed a car that Uncle Julian had kept away in storage and went over to the park. As I approached the center, I noticed Tyrik leaving Pitchoun! I stopped the car, wondering what he was up to when I saw Zuri come out a few seconds later. I became really curious as I stared at the two. She looked uneasy as Tyrik was saying something to her. I was going to get out of the car and go to them, but figured I shouldn't. I didn't want her to think that I had followed her there, so I continued to watch the scene, hoping I could figure out what was going on based on their body language. Besides, I did tell her to talk to him, but I didn't think it would have been this soon.

I watched as he put his arms around her for a hug. I waited to see if she'd return it. She leaned her body against him and gave a quick hug before going to our rental car.

I looked across the center and started back driving. After getting directions from the GPS, I was approaching the park. I immediately saw a black SUV parked nearby. I drove around near the SUV and parked in the lot. I got out and went near the park where Milo was sitting on a bench. He looked at me and smiled.

"I didn't think you would be here."

"I'm the one who should be saying that to you. I told you I was coming here," I said as I sat beside him.

"I know. You know I had to come and see if you made any progress."

"It's too early to tell."

"Looks like your girl has though. I saw her talking to little O'Neal. They looked mighty cozy. You should be scared about that."

"I don't have anything to worry about."

"Oh, do you? Enough about that. I have another job for you."

I looked ahead, clearly getting upset. I'm tired of being this man's lackey. It seemed as if he can't do anything for himself.

"What is it this time?"

"I need you to get rid of O'Neal's enforcer, that way he won't be in the way once you finally do get to Tyrik."

"He's not near Tyrik though. He's only around his dad, unless…"

Milo laughed. "I knew that college education would get you somewhere."

"Shit," I mumbled. "You want me to get rid of both Tyrik and Malcolm?"

"I have to in order for me to move into his territory. This is payback anyway for him trying to over step his boundaries."

"Milo, we had an agreement to get rid of Tyrik."

"I know, but I changed my mind. I want both of them dead within the next two weeks. If you don't deliver, then you, along with your girl will be the ones dead."

He stood up and stared at me. "You know, you're nothing like your parents. Those two were like puppets. They did exactly as I told them to do. You on the other hand, I have to continuously instruct. I don't have time or the patience to be repeating myself with you. Either do it or you're the one who will get dealt with."

I watched him leave before getting up. I was tired of this man and his damn instructions. If it was left up to me, I would have been arrested him or just killed him, but I have to go by the proper protocol so his charges will stick.

I went to Julian's car, eager to go back to the hotel to see what Zuri was up to.

***

Throughout the entire drive, I was thinking of how I should confront Zuri. I didn't want her to think I was following her, but I needed to know what she and Tyrik were talking about. Now that Milo wanted me to also kill Malcolm, I have to think long and hard on how I wanted to follow through with this.

I walked into the room and saw Zuri, along with Nicole and Chandler, which was a huge surprise to me.

"What are you two doing here?" I asked while going over to Chandler for a hug.

"Your uncle sent us here. We knew he was, but we didn't think it would be this soon," Chandler replied.

"I was just mentioning that to Z earlier this morning. That was when Chandler received the call from Julian."

"What about your parents?" I asked Chandler.

"They're here also. They're in another room at the hotel we're staying in."

"Is this safe for you to be here?"

"Yes it is, nephew," my uncle said while coming out of the bathroom. I looked at him and at Nicole and Chandler, realizing I had to wait to confront Zuri.

"They're going to have around the clock security as well as have aliases while they're here. They can't stay too long, that's why I brought them personally before they head back to their room."

Zuri glanced at me and noticed the look I had on my face. She gave a concerned one before talking to Nicole.

Chandler looked at me and sighed. "What's going on?"

"Nothing. Why do you think there is?"

"Because of that look. You always have that look when something is up."

"It's nothing, just have some things to figure out. Why didn't you tell me you were coming here?"

"It was a surprise. Your uncle didn't want anyone to know."

"And he's sure that you all are safe?"

"He wanted us to move around so no one would know our location. I'm fine with this since it is a free vacation."

"I'm sure, cheapskate."

Chandler laughed. "But all kidding aside, I really hope all of this blows over. I can tell Nicole is nervous about everything. That and she misses our home. I do too."

"I promise you unc and I will have this done and over with, trust me."

"I have no doubt that you will, D."

I nodded and he went over to Nicole and Zuri as Julian came over to me.

"So, how did it go?" he asked.

"There's no development on the case."

"How so?"

"Tyrik is not the only person Milo wants dead."

"Don't tell me his dad?"

"I don't know how much more of this I can take. I just want to live my life and not worry about whether I'll get arrested or shot at."

"Soon, all of this will be over. We just need a bit more evidence and potentially have him confess to some of the crime that has occurred, especially with Juan Diego's murder."

He looked at me and over at Zuri. "Did you want us to leave so you could talk to her?"

I folded my arms and shook my head. "No. Let them have their moment. My issues can wait."

I went over to Chandler, knowing I needed to spend time with my friend. I might not have another moment when I will.

Zuri

Spending time with Nicole and Chandler was so much fun. I missed being around them, but I knew their visit would be limited. Julian mentioned we would all have another time to meet up, but it would have to be spaced out, so it would be in the next couple of days.

Now Damon and I were sitting on the bed, watching TV. I looked at him as he was focused on the show that was on. He has been extremely quiet since everyone left, which kind of bothered me. I tried to touch him, and he pulled away, which really had me uneasy.

"Is everything okay, baby?"

He looked at me and turned back to the TV. "Now that you brought it up, no, it's not."

"What is it?"

He got up and went to the window before turning around to stare at me. "What were you doing with Tyrik today?"

"What?"

"Don't do that with me. What were you doing with him?"

"I was meeting him to get information out of him. Since I'm supposed to be anyway, I figured I might as well."

"But you didn't tell me about it."

"Oh, so you're my dad now and I have to tell you my every move? I don't even do that with my actual father."

"I'm only trying to look out for you. What if Tyrik was being followed? What if he's actually working for his father and put you in a trap? You have to be careful around him in case those things happen."

"He said the same thing about you."

"And you believed him?"

"Damon, I'm only trying to get to the truth."

"Just like I am, but you have to be careful of what you're doing to get to the truth."

I folded my arms across my chest and gave him a stern look. "Are you finished, Daddy?"

"I'm not playing, Zuri!"

I jumped, realizing he really wasn't. That was the first time I actually felt a little startled by him. He noticed the unsettled look I had as he came up to me.

"Baby, you know I'm only looking out for you. I don't want you to get hurt in this. Tyrik is bad news and his dad is even worse."

"Don't get me wrong, Damon, his dad is, but I think I believe Tyrik."

"What?"

"Sit down," I instructed and he sat on the bed.

"When I talked to him, he mentioned the alliance Malcolm had with Milo. He said that the two had a mutual agreement regarding their territories and that they would have equal shares. The thing is that Milo broke that alliance and went behind Malcolm's back to get out of it. That's why he overstepped his boundaries and this entire war between the two began. I really think Tyrik is telling the truth that Malcolm thought he was going to receive his rightful piece, but was screwed over."

Damon shook his head. "Honestly, he just might be. Milo is a sneaky bastard. But that doesn't mean I trust Malcolm either. He's known for being a con and a kiss ass to get what he wants. Tyrik could be saying the same thing to you."

"Maybe so, but from what I saw that day with Milo, I do believe what Tyrik said."

"Are you saying that you trust him?"

"I didn't say that, but I think we should look further into his accusations so we can get all the facts together."

"Okay, I'll take your word for it, but if anything happens…"

"I promise, we'll back off."

"You'll back off. I'll still be a part of it."

"You're being stubborn."

"And I'm used to this. I'm going to tell unc what you told me."

"You think it will help anything?"

"It might. We're just going to need back up when I talk to him."

I laughed. "No way. He won't tell you anything."

"He's going to have to. We have to find out what really happened and see if we can get the information we need."

"In that case, you might as tell him that Milo put a hit out on him."

"Not yet, but maybe if he tells me the right things, I will."

"You're playing with his life, Damon."

"Why are you so concerned about him? That guy called you all sorts of names and you still care about him."

"Despite the issues we had, he's innocent, and he shouldn't die because of his dad."

"You're right. No one should be punished for someone else's misdeeds, but what if he was working with his dad? I still say there's something off about that party. You said his dad hosted a ton of parties through your company. Why was it that night that shit started happening? You should really try to think hard about that night. Was anything different?"

"No, everything was normal."

"You sure nothing out of the ordinary was going on?"

"That I know of, no."

Damon sighed. "Okay, but if you think of anything, please let me know."

I nodded and he came over to give me a kiss. "We'll figure things out."

"I know."

He kissed me again and went to the kitchenette to grab some water. I sat down on the bed and stared ahead, going back to the night of the party. Everything was going well as I was monitoring the festivities. My mind continued to drift to different events of that night when something triggered in me. My eyes grew wide at the memory as I jumped up from the bed. Damon walked back and came over to me.

"Baby, what's wrong?"

I looked at him, feeling a bit startled. Since I didn't remember a lot of that night, this memory was surely one that I was surprised with.

"Talk to me, baby. What's wrong?"

"I remembered something."

Damon

Once Z told me she remembered something, I sat her down so she could think about that night. I wasn't going to rush her about this because this could be viable information on whether my suspicions were true about Malcolm playing a part to that night. Even though Milo is a deceitful bastard, the two are made from the same cloth, so he's capable of anything as well.

I watched as she had a blank look on her face. She looked at me and sighed.

"What do you remember?"

She looked scared, which was unlike her, so I knew this must be a big one.

"It was Malcolm who gave me the first drink. I remember talking to Erin and Tyrik when he came to me and asked if I wanted one. I kept telling him no since I was working, but he insisted, saying that this was his party and he wanted everyone, including us, to have fun. Tyrik insisted as well, but Malcolm was so pushy. It was as if he needed me to take that drink."

"Do you remember anything else?"

She shook her head. "No. I'm surprised I remembered that."

"So after that first drink, do you know if he was giving you more, or was that when the craziness started?"

"It could have been, but I do know I had more than the drink he gave me."

"For all we know, he could have spiked it. I'm glad you're able to remember that much. That'll be a good way for us to piece together some of the events, and maybe see a connection to them."

"I hope so."

"In the meantime, I'm still going to talk to Tyrik. Do you know where he could be right now?"

"Possibly at the office."

"Are you going to be okay here?"

"Yes, but I really don't think you should talk to him. Not right now, anyway."

"I'm just going to have a civil conversation with him. There won't be any altercations, if that's what you're worried about."

"Okay. Even though I don't want you doing it, I know you're going to."

"Yeah, I am. Text me the office address so I'll have it."

"Sure."

I grabbed the keys to the rental and left. There're a lot of things I wanted to discuss with Tyrik. Hopefully I'll be able to without wanting to bash his head in.

***

After I left the room, Zuri texted me the address, which was in the area of the hotel. I parked in the garage and went to the entrance where I saw Erin talking with someone. She looked over and saw me, waving her hand to come over. I went over, not wanting to talk to her, but I didn't want to be rude.

"What are you doing here?" she asked.

"Just in the area. Is Tyrik here?"

"He is, but why are you asking, Damon? I really hope you're not going to make a scene at our place of business."

"Would I do that? I'm only going to have a civil conversation with him. So why don't you go back to whatever you were doing and mind your own business, okay?"

Erin gave me a surprised look as I walked off. I don't see how Zuri was able to work with her.

Instead of asking her where Tyrik's office was, I asked security, who directed me there. I didn't even knock as I walked in, seeing him, along with his dad sitting on the couch. That took me by surprise because I wasn't trying to talk to him too.

"How did you get in here?" Tyrik asked.

"Security. You probably should hire someone who doesn't just let anyone in."

"You probably gave him a lame ass story. Now I'll call them to escort you out."

"Why so sudden? I only wanted to talk to you about an important matter."

"I don't want to talk to you."

"I'm sure you do if it involves Zuri."

He looked at me and I smiled. "I guess that got your attention."

Malcolm looked at me and smiled. "Aren't you Damon Baxter, one of Milo's employees? You used to work for him, correct?"

"He still does," Tyrik mumbled.

"Yes, I did. I definitely know you, Malcolm O'Neal. You and Milo had an alliance at one point. What happened to that?"

"I'm sure you know since you used to work for Milo. Your boss screwed me over."

I folded my arms across my chest. "You sure you didn't do anything to piss him off? Milo is the type of person who doesn't take betrayal kindly."

"You should know that quite well, Mr. Baxter, especially since you quit on him. Or did you?"

I looked at Tyrik who gave an evil smirk. I ought to go over to him and knock it off of him.

"That's not really any of your concern, Mr. O'Neal. Besides, I'm not here to talk about my former boss, I'm here to talk to your son about Zuri."

"Whatever you have to say, you can do so in front of my father."

I took a deep breath and stood in front of Tyrik. "I know about your conversation with her earlier. What were you two talking about?"

"That conversation was between me and Zuri. Like you told my father, that's not your concern."

"It is my concern if it involves my girlfriend. Now, what were you two talking about?"

"You are with Zuri now? Wow, time definitely has changed," Malcolm said and smiled.

I looked at Tyrik and he sighed. "It wasn't nothing important, we were talking about the time we were together, that's all."

"I don't think that was the conversation. In fact, I think it had a lot to do with the alliance that your father had with Milo and how it backfired. Now, should I be protective of myself and Zuri if another turf war goes into effect?"

"Shouldn't you be asking your boss that? He's the one who's always so damn trigger happy. Oh wait, I forgot, he's not the one who pulls the trigger on anything. That's what he has you for," Malcolm said.

"You're right, I was his lackey. Hell, I still am, but I'm good at what I do. I'm sure your hired men know a thing or two about that, especially Oliver, who's nursing that broken hand. If he or that punk assed friend of his come after Zuri or me again, that hand won't be the only thing that will be a concern."

"If you do anything to my men, then that's on you. I can always hire more help," Malcolm said while taking a seat on the couch.

"The real reason why I'm here is to talk about that party you threw that cost Zuri her job. I need to know was she drugged."

Tyrik glanced at me as if I was crazy. "What? You're really grasping at straws."

"No, I think I'm on to something. A lot of things are not adding up and in my opinion, I think either you or your daddy over there did something to harm Zuri. Maybe she was on to something about one of you or you just did it for kicks, but regardless, you ruined a woman's reputation to further your damn agenda."

Tyrik still looked speechless as he looked at his dad. His expression was calm as he straightened out his tie.

"I think I hit a nerve because little O'Neal looks as if he's about to shit on himself. So tell me, which one of my theories is correct?"

"None of them, Mr. Baxter. There's nothing to solve. Zuri had too much to drink and didn't know how to handle herself. Plain and simple."

"I get it, she did go too far, but there was a reason for her going to that point. I think you had something to do with that, especially since you were the one giving her drinks."

Malcolm still had that stupid ass smirk on his face while I studied Tyrik. He didn't look too happy, so either he's pissed that I knew about that, or he really was unaware of that bit of news.

"I don't know what Zuri told you, but that night she clearly had a lot of fun. I mean, the pictures and the video show that. She's bitter because she got caught."

"No, she's worried that there was a bigger agenda behind this and whether her life is in danger right now."

"Her life is in danger regardless, especially since she's with you, Damon," Tyrik said.

"Maybe so, but there's something that you two are hiding and I'm not going to rest until I find out," I said and went to the door. I turned around to stare at them.

"And if you try to hire anyone to come after the two of us, just know that I'll be ready for them."

I turned around and went to the door, knowing that those two had something to do with that night. I just hope I can find the proof I need to get rid of them as well as get revenge on Milo.

Zuri

I stared out the window, wondering when Damon was returning. He has been gone quite a while, so hopefully he didn't run into any trouble with Tyrik. I received a text from Erin letting me know that he was at the office asking for Tyrik. Of course I played the dumbfounded routine, letting her know I had nothing to do with that and he probably looked him up online in regards to the office.

I wanted to call Nicole and tell her everything that was happening when the door opened and Damon walked in. I went up to him and gave him a hug.

"What did you find out?"

"Nothing. Daddy O'Neal was there so of course Tyrik wasn't going to say anything. But I think I scared him a bit about the party."

"What do you mean?"

"When I told them about Malcolm giving you drinks, he was being nonchalant about it while Tyrik was nervous. I really think he was working with his father to expose you, Z."

"But why? I didn't even know anything about him or Milo at the time."

"You sure Tyrik didn't tell you anything about the business between the two? Maybe he slipped up or you caught them doing something."

"No, Malcolm was very discreet about everything. I'm sorry, babe, but I don't know anything."

"That's okay. Like I mentioned, at least you were able to piece together about him giving you drinks."

"I don't know how I was able to forget that."

"Your memory was lost about that night, which I believed they wanted to happen so you wouldn't uncover the truth."

"So you really think this is all connected?"

"I have no doubt that it is. I just need the proof to uncover it."

I sighed and realized I was getting hungry. I was tired of ordering room service and just wanted to go out. I gave him a pleading look as he was unsure of what I was hinting at.

"What?"

"Are you hungry, because I definitely am."

"We can always order room service."

"Or we can go out for a quick bite. Just to this diner I know and we can come back."

"Z, I really don't think we should go out. Now that you met with Tyrik and Milo is here…"

"Milo is here! When did you see him?"

"Earlier today. Don't worry, he doesn't know where we are, which I would like to keep that way."

"It's just dinner. What could possibly happen?"

"Anything can happen, Z."

I sighed and gave him another pleading look. He shook his head and grabbed the keys.

"Thirty minutes. We're getting our food to go."

"Sounds like a plan. Besides, if anything goes down, I have my faith in you to kick some ass."

"You will also, right?"

"Of course, babe."

He opened the door and led me out first. Nothing could go wrong in thirty minutes, right?

***

Once I gave him directions on where to go, we were at Pink's picking up their famous hot dogs. I couldn't be in L.A. and not experience one of these things. That would be wrong of me if I did.

Before going back to the hotel, we had to stop and get some gas. I was in the car while Damon was at the pump. I wanted to get some ice cream, so I got out and walked inside. I looked at a couple of things before going to the freezer section and opening it to grab a pint of rocky road. As soon as I closed the door, I looked outside and saw a sight that I didn't want to see.

"Damon!" I yelled, throwing down the ice cream and running out of the store. I ran near the car when someone grabbed me from behind. I was struggling with the guy while I watched two men jump Damon. He tried to fight them off of him, but he was outnumbered. I couldn't stand there and do nothing. I had to help him.

I jabbed my elbow into the guy's stomach and kicked my foot backwards to hit him in the shin. I turned around and hit him, causing him to fall down. Before I could go to Damon, the guy grabbed me again and was trying to throw me on the ground when a shot was fired. I looked behind me and saw Damon with his gun pointed at the guy. The other two guys he was fighting with before were laid out on the ground.

"Now you see why I said we should have ordered room service? That was O'Neal's men trying to scare us."

"How do you know that?"

"Because I threatened the son of a bitch earlier. I guess this was his message that he was coming after us."

"I'm really sorry, Damon."

"It's fine. We need to go though. I'm sure the worker called the cops."

I nodded as we went to the car, but before we could get inside, a shot was fired, causing both of us to fall down. Another shot rang out as I went behind the door, shielding myself while shots were continuing to go off. Once it was done, I heard tires squealing as I looked behind me. A crowd was forming as some were looking at the other guys that were near the pump. But the person I was concerned with was laying near the car, which had my heart going wild.

"Damon!" I yelled as I went to him. I slightly moved him to see he was shot in the chest.

"Oh my God! Someone help me!" I yelled as someone ran over to me.

My heart started to break in two at the sight of him. I can't believe this was happening. I knew this would be a risk, but not only is Damon a cop, he's also a hitman. He's usually the one shooting, not the one being shot at.

The person helping me mentioned he was a doctor, which was a relief, but it didn't ease my mind at all. I went to get my phone from the car to call Julian to let him know what happened. I had to stay distracted because I didn't want to see Damon that way.

While I waited for him to answer, I took several deep breaths, thinking of what I should do. Although Damon wanted me to be less involved as possible, I realized that I'm in this more than he wanted me to. Not only were they after him, but me as well. I take that very personally.

Now, I wasn't going to be a damn victim like I was that night at Malcolm's party. Whether it was Milo or Malcolm, if they wanted a fight, then they got one now. I'm not backing down from anything or anyone.

Now, I'm ready to seek revenge.

Zuri

I stood motionless in the emergency room at Cedars-Sinai Medical Center, not knowing if Damon was okay. The doctor that was at the gas station was able to stabilize him, but he was still unconscious from the time he was there to when he was transported to the hospital.

"Zuri, you need to sit, standing is not going to help Damon."

I turned around and stared at Julian. He quickly came to the gas station after I called him. He wanted to take me to the hospital, but I rode in the ambulance.

"I'm fine, Julian."

"He's right, Z."

I looked at Nicole who was there with Chandler. She was consoling him while he had his head down.

"This is part of the job, Zuri. We all know that Damon will pull through. He has before."

I gave Julian a wide-eyed stare. That was something else Damon failed to tell me.

"He has been shot before?"

"It was during a shooting with someone Milo wanted killed. Even though Damon shot the guy, he didn't know someone else was lurking around waiting for him. He was shot in the back," Chandler said.

"And this is okay? He could die!"

"Yes, he can, but we all know that Damon is a fighter. He doesn't back down from anything, including surviving. He's going to pull through, Zuri," Julian assured me.

Nicole came over to me and guided me to the nearest seat to sit down.

"I was there and saw all of the blood he lost. He looked so helpless," I whispered.

Nicole put an arm around me. I wasn't going to cry. I didn't want to. I looked at Nicole as she wiped the tears from her cheeks.

"Thank you and Chandler for being here, but should you both be here?"

Julian nodded. "We have plain clothed cops around the wing and outside. They'll handle everything, Zuri."

We continued to wait for two hours when a doctor walked out of the emergency wing. I quickly jumped up, knowing it was news about Damon.

"Baxter family."

"Yes, I'm his uncle. How is he?" Julian asked while coming next to me.

"First, I want to introduce myself. I'm Dr. Westbourne and I have been treating Damon since he arrived. He was shot twice, with one of the bullets going through his chest and the other was a superficial wound to his shoulder. With the emergency surgery, we were successfully able to get the bullet from his chest."

I didn't even know he went into surgery when I looked at Julian. He wasn't even surprised by that. He must have authorized it without us knowing.

"Damon will need his rest, possibly two to three weeks, so he can't do any type of strenuous activities whatsoever."

"We understand, doctor, and he won't," Julian acknowledged.

"Can we see him?" I asked.

"He's still asleep from the anesthesia, but if you would like, someone can stay in his room."

"Go, Zuri," Julian said.

I smiled and followed Dr. Westbourne through the ER double doors. We went through the corridor and to the elevators, which he mentioned they just moved Damon to ICU. Once we left the elevator, Dr. Westbourne went to the first room and opened the door. My heart dropped at the sight of Damon lying in the hospital bed. That was a sight I never wanted to see.

"I'll let you have some time. There are some blankets in the closet near the restroom for you to use."

"Thank you, Dr. Westbourne."

"No problem," he said as I went to the side of the bed. I watched him as he was asleep. His vitals were steady as I glanced at the machines. I went over to the closet and grabbed a blanket and went back to the chair. I sat down and draped it over me, hoping that Damon will wake up soon.

***

June 2015

"Are the caterers set-up? How about the DJ?" I asked through my Bluetooth headset. I walked around the ballroom of The Redbury, surveying the area, making sure everything was perfect for our huge event. Tyrik's dad, Malcolm O'Neal, was throwing a huge event for his new line of vodka that would launch soon. Even though Malcolm always threw parties through Randall Promotions, this one was a pretty big deal.

I went to the bar when I felt a pair of hands go across my waist. I couldn't help but to smile as his lips touched my neck.

"You know you shouldn't be showing affection here."

"Like it matters. This is my dad's event, remember?"

"And that's supposed to mean something?"

"It means I can do whatever I damn well want," he whispered and he nibbled on my ear.

"You better not let Randall hear you say that?"

Tyrik smiled. "So, you haven't answered my question."

"About what?"

"About our wedding. We still haven't set a date."

"I know and I'm getting to that. I've just been busy."

"I've been busy too, but I've been thinking about getting married. We've been at this for months and I feel as if we're still getting nowhere with planning."

"Why are you bringing this up here?"

"Because you never have time to talk about it anywhere else."

"I have a job to do," I said and walked past him. I went to Erin, who gave a slight smile.

"I see you and Tyrik are at it again."

"He's just asking about the wedding."

"Which I'm sure it's about the date. You shouldn't let him wait, Zuri."

"I'm not, it's just—"

"It's about your ex, isn't it? You're still hung up on Damon."

"It's not that."

"Then what is it? You have a great guy in Tyrik, yet you're still thinking about a man that you walked out on five years ago. Does he know about the baby?"

"No, he doesn't."

Erin shook her head and straightened a few plates before staring at me. "I really hope you get your priorities straight. You might lose Tyrik too."

I leaned against the table, knowing she was right. I care about Tyrik, but I'm not sure if I was in love with him. He was completely different from Damon, which was great for me. I didn't have to worry if I would get shot or shot at. That's the type of stability I was looking for in my life.

Once I did another walkthrough, I looked over and saw Erin and Tyrik talking in the corner. She was being super flirty as she put her hand on his chest. She slowly rubbed him before smiling and walked away.

I looked at Tyrik who was wearing a huge grin before going down the corridor. I took a deep breath, wondering what the hell that was about. I was about to follow him when Randall came to me asking about the final guest list.

I guess my concerns would have to wait.

***

Two hours later and the party was going pretty hard. So much was going on that it was hard for me to monitor everything. I was near the food, about to quickly grab an Hors D'oeuvre when a hand went across mine. I looked over and saw Malcolm standing beside me.

"Once again, you did a great job, Zuri."

I smiled. "I can't take all of the credit. The entire team did wonderful, including your son."

"He always has been hard working and driven. Takes after his old man."

"I can imagine."

"Why aren't you enjoying yourself? You put this together, so you should at least have a few minutes of fun."

"So Randall can fire me? No thanks."

"Come on, you know the person who the party is for, so you're cool."

"Malcolm..."

"Come on, one drink."

I stared at him as he got a shot of vodka from Erin and handed it to me. I glanced at her as she gave a sweet smile.

"Drink up, you deserve it, Z."

I looked from her to Malcolm, who gave a pearly white smile.

"One drink won't hurt, will it?"

I took the glass from Erin and started to drink. Even though I shouldn't, it felt good going down my throat. This was something that I needed.

Besides, they were right, one drink wouldn't hurt.

***

An hour later and four shots of vodka, and I was feeling the effects. Not only was I dancing, eating, and took a couple of topless pictures in the restroom. I was feeling so horny that I had to fuck Tyrik in one of the stalls of the men's restroom. Not one of my proudest moments, but he didn't seem to mind. When I wanted to loosen up earlier, I didn't think it would be like this.

I stumbled towards the coat closet, glancing at my surroundings, when I noticed Erin standing inside with Malcolm. The two glanced at me and smiled.

"I see you finally made it," Erin said and giggled.

"I needed a moment alone. What's going on? Why are you two in here?"

"We were waiting for you, Zuri," Malcolm said.

"Is it okay if I rest? I'm not feeling well," I said and sat down on the bench near the rack of coats.

"Maybe we can make you feel better," Erin said. She came over to me as I tried to keep my eyes open. She started touching my hair as Malcolm approached me. It was hard for me to stay awake as his hand caressed my shoulder. I didn't know what the hell was going on, but I knew I needed to do something.

"What are you two doing?"

"You're beautiful, Zuri. Don't you know that?" Malcolm asked.

He tried to put his hand on my thigh, but I pushed it away. I tried to get up, but instead, fell down to the floor.

I had to get away from these two, but my body wouldn't let me. Regardless, I had to fight, which I did so by grabbing an umbrella nearby and swinging it at the two. I went to the door, still trying to hit them so they would back away from me.

Before leaving out, I felt a rip going through my dress, but it didn't matter. I went down the hall, trying to get away from them as much as possible, when my knees grew weak. I made it to the hallway before collapsing by a hotel room. That was when everything faded to black.

I quickly woke up and looked around, realizing I was still in Damon's hospital room. I looked over and saw him looking at me. He looked groggy from the surgery and the medication as he slowly blinked.

"Are you okay?" he whispered.

I got up and went to him. "I should be asking you that."

"You know I am. Two bullets are not going to slow me down," he said and gave a slight grin.

"They definitely won't."

"You looked startled."

"I'm fine. It was just a bad dream."

"You want to talk about it?" he asked, trying to get up, but he slowly laid back down.

"Don't, Damon. You just had surgery, so you need to rest."

"If something is bothering you, then I would like to know."

I smiled. "You will in time, Damon. Right now, just focus on getting better."

He slowly nodded and gently grabbed my hand. He looked into my eyes as I slowly laid in bed with him. I gave him a kiss on the forehead as I tried to go back to sleep, but with what I just dreamt, that was going to be hard to do.

Zuri

After only getting a couple hours of sleep, it was morning, and I was in the waiting room waiting on Dr. Westbourne to finish examining Damon. The doctor didn't want me in, so I respected his privacy.

I tried to keep my attention on a cooking show on TV, when my mind kept wandering to the dream I had earlier. Now I was able to remember the details to what happened, but I was still puzzled to what happened after I blacked out. For all I knew, Malcolm could have still done something, which was making me feel ill.

And Erin; I guess her taking my position when I was ousted was her motive for going along with whatever Malcolm had cooked up. He had equal share in the company, so he could have done anything to get what he wanted.

"What are you thinking about?"

I looked over and stared at Nicole, who handed me a cup of coffee.

"Remember I told you I remembered Malcolm giving me a drink? Well, I dreamt the entire event earlier. It was Erin who gave me that shot of vodka, but I believed Malcolm put her up to it."

"Why?"

"To get my job. He probably figured that was a way to use her."

"But what really happened?"

"They tried to rape me."

"They?"

"Yes, they. You know Erin goes both ways, so that wouldn't have bothered her at all."

"Wow, so how were you able to get away?"

"I used an umbrella as a weapon, but I collapsed in the hallway. Everything after that is a blank."

"Wow, but where were you when you came to?"

"In one of the rooms. I remembered Tyrik renting one for the night."

"Do you think he was in on it?"

"Right now, I don't know what to believe. What would be the motive for Malcolm doing this? Like I told Damon, I didn't even know he was a crime boss until I got involved with him again."

"But how do you know they didn't know about you? I'm sure Malcolm did a check on you since you were with his son."

"I was thinking that, but there has to be another reason behind this. Evidently, Malcolm was trying to get rid of me."

"You never stumbled upon any information about him, have you?"

I shook my head. "Not that I know of. I rarely seen him but at his parties."

I glanced at Nicole, who gave me a curious look.

"What's wrong?"

"Wow," I said and put my head in my hands.

"What's going on?"

"Now I know why he drugged me. There was this event that he was having. I remember I had to look for him to ask a question about the guest list. I was about to walk into the conference room, but I stopped because he was in the middle of a meeting. I stood there, waiting on them to finish, when he pulled out a gun and shot the person in the chest. I was so shocked that I just stood there, not able to move. I heard yelling and then my eyes locked with Malcolm's. That's when I left."

"Do you know who the person was or who else was there?"

I shook my head. "Milo was there. I didn't think of it at the time because I didn't know who he was. As for the person who was shot dead, I have no idea."

"You know I told you about Erin. That girl looked sneaky as hell. I know Damon had his suspicions too."

"He sort of did. And I was going to help her plan a new party for Malcolm."

"Who said you shouldn't?"

"I don't know if I can be around her."

"You're going to have to if you want to expose Malcolm. Was that the agreement you had with Damon?"

"Which he'll understand."

"Zuri, don't you want to fight for everything that has happened to you? These people took your life, so you should want to do what you can to take it back."

"What if they both go after my family? After you and Chandler? I wouldn't know what to do if they did."

"Z, you have been targeted by those things for years now, even more so now, because you're with Damon. Do you want to keep hiding out, not living your life?"

"No, but—"

"Stop! I know you have been through a lot recently, but I know you're stronger than this."

I sighed and pulled out my phone. I went to my photo app and handed it to Nicole.

"What am I looking at?" she asked.

"Since I've been helping Damon, I decided to do a little digging of my own. I was able to learn a little about Damon's parents and how involved they were with Milo, even though the relationship was very dysfunctional."

"Had to have been if his mom was involved with Milo," Nicole said and shivered.

"I think it was more than that. Yes, she had an affair, but I think the two were doing a lot more than sleeping with each other."

"You think they were seeking revenge on someone?"

I shrugged. "I don't know, but the story doesn't make sense."

"Are you going to tell Damon?"

I sighed. "Not until I get proof. I don't want to jump the gun on anything, especially if I don't have the right info."

Nicole nodded and I looked ahead, knowing I shouldn't be keeping more information from Damon, but with his parents, I had to. Not just for him, but for everyone around him.

Damon

Once Dr. Westbourne checked my vitals, he informed me that everything looked good, but I would still be in the hospital for a few more days. I really wanted to jump back into the case, but I couldn't, which could put a strain on a lot of things, including with Milo. Although I didn't tell him I was shot, I have a feeling that he knows.

The door opened and Chandler walked in. I gave him a small smile as he came over to the bed. "I saw your doctor and he told me it was fine to come in. Where's Zuri?"

"In the waiting room. Dr. Westbourne told her to step out while he examined me."

"Oh, she's probably with Nicole then. So, how are things looking for you?"

"Better, but I still need to recover."

"Which I can expect. You know Zuri was frantic over you, especially when she discovered this wasn't the first time you were shot."

"I know she was, that's why I didn't tell her. But there's something she hasn't told me."

"What do you mean?"

"I think she remembers what happened to her at Malcolm's party."

"Why do you think that?"

"I was up for an hour last night. I was still groggy, but I couldn't go back to sleep. I watched her toss and turn for a good fifteen minutes before she jumped up and looked at me. She didn't want to tell me, but I knew that was the reason."

"That could have been anything though."

"Maybe so, but it was the look on her face. It was a mix of being scared and anger. She knew what happened, but didn't want to tell me."

"She didn't because you are recovering from a gunshot wound. Be grateful that she cares enough not to tell you."

"But she shouldn't be withholding things from me. We agreed that we shouldn't after our last talk."

"Just like you haven't with your plan about your parents."

I sighed. "I only did that to protect her. The less she knows, the better, especially if my theory is true. Thank you by the way for digging up my parents' history."

"You know I would have done it, but you need to tell her what you're doing. That way, she can be prepared for what will happen. She shouldn't be kept in the dark, Damon."

"I know and I shouldn't. I'll talk to her once she returns."

"You never know. She might bring up her dream."

"Let's hope so. But have you found out anything new?"

Chandler nodded and pulled out his phone. "I took a couple of pictures of the files I obtained from the police department. With Escobar's murder, it looked as if your dad killed him, but based on his autopsy, there was also potassium chloride found in his blood."

"That means he was dying anyway. Someone poisoned him."

"And covered it up with your dad shooting him."

"Wow. I knew Milo was deceitful, but to do that is crazy."

"There's something else, D."

He scrolled through the phone to show another file. I looked at it as he leaned back in his seat.

"With the accident, you already knew it was deliberate, but I doubt Milo was the one who was behind it."

"What do you mean?"

"I think you need to look at your uncle. There's a lot more to the story than he's letting on."

I continued to look at the image, reading what was there, but not making any sense of it. I'm a cop, so I should be able to. Or maybe I didn't want to.

"I'm really sorry, D. I wish I had better news."

I slowly gave back his phone and stared ahead. This was starting to become too much. When I took on my own investigation, I expected for a lot to happen, but not like this. Now, the person that had raised me since my parents' death could have had a part in their demise.

Zuri

I was nervous as I rounded the corner to Damon's room. My hands started to sweat while my breathing became ragged. I didn't know if I was going to tell him about what I discovered, but I knew I had to. I was holding the secret about me having an abortion, so I figured I needed to clear my conscience on the other secret.

I knocked on the door as Damon said to come in. I slowly walked in as he looked over at me and smiled.

"Hey baby. I was wondering when you were coming back."

"Sorry I took so long. Nicole mentioned that Chandler walked up here so I figured you and him were talking."

"Sit down," he instructed and I nodded as I walked over to the chair by the bed. I slowly sat down and stared at him. He gave me a concerned look, wondering what was going on.

"If you need to talk, then you can. What's going on?"

I took a deep breath to calm myself before speaking. "Remember last night when you saw me a bit distracted."

"Yeah. Something was wrong. Did you dream about the party?"

"Yeah. It was definitely something I didn't want to relive, that's probably why I blocked it from my memory."

I continued to talk, giving Damon the details to what happened. He sighed, shaking his head, not believing what he was hearing.

"Wow. I knew I couldn't trust Erin. In my line of work, the first impression is always critical, and she was horrible."

"I don't think I can help her with the party."

"You should, that's the only way you're going to get information about Tyrik and Malcolm."

"That's what Nicole said."

"You told her before me?"

"I wasn't trying to. I didn't think I should have because you might not have taken it well."

"You see me now? I'm calm as ever."

"That's because you're in a hospital bed and you can't do anything."

"I still can."

"And your condition will become worse."

"Now I have even more of a reason to kill Malcolm."

"Haven't you done enough killing, Damon? Trust me, I want to see Malcolm get what he deserves, but in the right way. You have to be above Milo and use your badge to get rid of Malcolm."

"Has my badge really helped anything? All it has done was put me into even further shit. Now, I'm putting the law into my hands and that's starting with Milo, Malcolm, and possibly my own damn uncle."

I gave him a puzzled look as he stared at the blank TV ahead. "What does that mean?"

"I haven't told you, but I asked Chandler to dig up my parents' past. He has found out some pretty interesting things regarding the events leading up to them being killed."

"Like what?"

"With Escobar, he was poisoned with potassium chloride, so the gunshot wound wasn't the cause of his murder. Also, with the accident, the SUV didn't lose control, it was pushed off thc road."

"What? How did Chandler find all of this out?"

"He hacked into the police department's files. Even though they were sealed, he found a way to go into them."

"But since you're a cop, why were you never able to know about this?"

"Because of Uncle Julian. He was the one covering it up. Every time I tried to gain access to public records, files, what have you, he wouldn't let me."

"Wow. Are you saying that Julian was a part of it?"

"Yeah, I really think he was. As for his motive, I wouldn't know why."

"There's something else I need to tell you, it's also about your parents."

Damon was curious as I continued.

"You weren't the only one who was digging. I decided to do some research as well. What you learned, I kind of already knew. As for your uncle, I really didn't know that. If he is a part of it, why would you think he would do it?"

"Who knows. Either he might have known something with Milo and my parents besides the affair, or there's something else lurking that no one wants out."

"Wow, babe. I really thought your uncle was legit."

"He could be, but there's probably something that he's hiding. But let's go back to you. If you said you and Tyrik had sex in the men's room, how were you two recorded?"

That was the part I was wondering as I tried to figure that part out. Unless there was one person who could have been involved.

"There are two options. One is Erin could have recorded us, the second option is also Erin recording us, but either Malcolm or Tyrik had her to do it."

"Which means that Tyrik would have been involved in it."

"Yes, unfortunately."

"How is that unfortunate? He's just like his daddy."

"Maybe because I know the other side to him. The side that I've been seeing since I returned is not him. Even at the party, he wasn't acting like himself. Something is going on. For all we know, he could have been forced into it."

"You're giving him more credit than he's worth. What I saw the day in his office was the second coming of Malcolm O'Neal. For all you know, he could have put a hit out on both of us, just like him and his dad tried to do at 90 West Lounge."

"Yes, his dad could have."

"But not Tyrik? You're being delusional if you think he's not involved in this."

"I really don't think he is, Damon."

"Why are you defending him? He could have been the one to order to kill us, but you think he's this upstanding guy. Zuri, right now, everyone is guilty until proven innocent. Hell, even my uncle is on the damn list."

I looked down at the linoleum floor, knowing that Damon was right. At one point, I thought Erin was innocent until I had my dream. Now, she's on top of the list of people not to trust.

"Okay, he is too. I'll try to keep my composure when I'm working with Erin, and even Tyrik. I know I will have to watch those two carefully."

"Yes, you do. Baby, I just want you to have an open mind, but also stay on guard with who you're associating with. There could be a lot of things that are still out there that could hurt both of us. So, just be careful."

I nodded. "I understand, especially now. I'm supposed to be meeting with Erin later today to go over a couple of decorations. I was thinking about bringing Nicole, if you think that's cool."

"You probably have to. I'll call Uncle Julian to have plain clothed officers around you three."

"You think that's a good idea to ask your uncle?"

He shrugged. "I have to keep the charade going. I can't back off now or he'll know something is up."

"Okay."

"But get ready for your meeting. I'll be here."

I smiled and kissed him before getting up.

"Have you talked to your parents?"

"I actually have. They're having fun, especially my dad."

"Wow, I guess this did work out well for them."

"At least they're having fun and not worried about getting shot at," I said. Damon smirked as I walked out of the room. Now it was time to put on my good face and meet up with Erin. At least I'll have Nicole there because I know eventually, I would hurt Erin.

***

Once Nicole met me at the hospital, we drove to Calabasas to meet with Erin. I was getting excited with the idea of working again. I missed planning events and seeing them come to life. I hope once all of this blows over I can regain my life back and find another job in the field.

"You sure you're going to be comfortable doing this?"

"I have to be. This is not just for myself, but also for Damon."

We got to the venue and saw Erin and Tyrik standing near the door. I looked at Nicole and sighed.

"Let's get this over with."

Nicole got out of the car and stared at the two. Tyrik rolled his eyes at the sight of her.

"Why are you here?"

"I came to support my friend. Besides, she needs sane people around her compared to the people that she has hung around."

Tyrik looked at me and smiled. "I'm glad you came."

"You all needed my help, so let's get started. As for Nicole being here, I asked her to come. The more, the merrier, right?"

"Fine, but only if she gives great ideas. I know you Nicole and you don't have any taste," Tyrik said.

"You really are an idiot."

"We're not going to do this right now! Instead, we're going to plan this party. Since I'm working for free, I can pretty much bring who I want, so no shit starting, are we clear?" I demanded.

"Whatever," Tyrik mumbled. I gave him the death stare, which he should know all so well. Erin didn't say anything as she walked ahead of us to the venue. She better not had.

Tyrik walked up to the door and opened it, revealing a beautifully spaced venue. We surveyed the area, trying to get ideas on what would go where. Since Malcolm was doing a launch party for his new record label, the space would have to have a stage so his artists can do their performances. I have to hand it to him, even though he's a criminal, he's also a smart business man.

Tyrik looked around and nodded. "This place is perfect. I can imagine us having a great time here."

"Definitely. I love the structure. I can imagine the sound here will be incredible," Erin agreed.

I looked at Nicole who had a bored look on her face.

"This shit is boring," she whispered. I gave her the death stare too as I watched Erin and Tyrik. Nicole wasn't into designing or planning, so I expected this from her.

"Why are you here again?" Erin asked.

"You need to mind your business."

"But you're in the way of us getting anything done. I wasn't going to say anything Zuri, but how are you going to be taken seriously again in this industry if you're bringing strays with you to important meetings?"

"Who in the hell are you calling a stray? I'm not a damn animal," Nicole fumed.

"You're kind of acting like one now."

I dug my nails into Nicole's arm. I knew she'll pop off soon, so hopefully I can prevent her from doing so.

"You have a lot of nerve talking about anyone when you're going around acting like a damn hoe. That was Zuri's job that you're comfortably doing. Your no talent ass had to scheme and fuck to get it."

"Wow, classy, Nicole," Tyrik said.

"Let her talk since she knows me so well," Erin said.

"I know about people like you. You're nothing but a snake, especially with all the backstabbing you have done to Zuri."

"I can speak for myself, you know," I whispered to Nicole.

"I know, but I had to get that off my chest. Smug assed bitch."

"Okay, I'm not working under these conditions. Either she goes or I do."

"No one is going anywhere, but there is one thing that I need to know," I stepped in.

Nicole folded her arms across her chest and gave Erin a smirk.

"It's game time now, bitch."

"Really, Nicole," Tyrik said.

"Oh, this involves you too, pretty boy."

I sighed and looked at Erin. "I wasn't going to bring this up, but since Nicole got the ball rolling, I'll go ahead. Did you set me up that night at the party?"

Erin looked surprised as she put a hand to her chest. Nicole rolled her eyes.

"Answer the question!" she exclaimed.

"Do you really think that I would? If so, then you really don't know me."

"I thought I did, but I'm starting to see things a lot clearer now."

"I assure you, I had nothing to do with that."

"Do you think we're stupid, Erin? Whatever you gave her didn't make her lose her memory," Nicole said.

"I don't have to take this," she said while walking away, but I grabbed her arm.

"I know what you and Malcolm did. Someone drugged me and both of you tried to take advantage of me."

"I don't know what you're talking about."

I twisted her arm, making her wince. I looked into her eyes, hoping I'll get a confession soon.

"Tell the truth, Erin. Was it you that did it, or were you forced to by Malcolm?"

"Hold up, my dad wouldn't have done that," Tyrik said.

"You're kidding, right? He'll do anything to get what he wants. You could have been a part of the plan, too."

"I didn't know anything about what happened."

"But you know what happened after though. I was in the hotel room that you rented for the night."

"Yes, because I found you passed out in the hallway. I carried you to the room and put you in the bed."

"What made you look down the hallway though?" Nicole asked.

"Why are we talking about this right now? I really don't think this was a good idea to include you, Zuri. In fact, you and her can go," Erin said and pointed at Nicole.

"Not until I find out the truth. There are too many stories, but I haven't heard the correct one. I need answers to what happened to me!"

"Alright! I was the one who videoed the two of you as well as leaked the video."

I shook my head at Erin who sighed.

"What! How could you do that?!" Tyrik exclaimed.

"Because I wanted Zuri's job. I was with the company way longer than you and to have been under you was a slap in the face! That should have been my title from the start!"

"Yet, you destroyed my life in the process. Do you feel good about that?"

"Actually, I do."

I went up to her and punched her in her mouth, causing her to fall back onto a metal table.

"You thug!" she yelled.

I grabbed her hair, causing her to look at me.

"You know, I could kill you right now. Hell, my man's a hitman, so he's always ready to mark someone."

"Do you really want to go there? He may be a hitman, but I know higher people in higher places."

"So do I, bitch!"

I pushed her face into the metal table, hitting her.

“Zuri, stop!” Tyrik yelled, but I didn’t listen to him. I kept banging her face against the table, making her feel the hurt and pain that I went through when I was publicly humiliated. I felt Nicole near me as she pulled me away from Erin. She stared at her, and her face was covered with blood.

"I know you want to hurt her, but you're going to need her to get into that party. Also, she hasn’t explained the entire story, which you will right now, right Erin?”

“This is crazy,” Tyrik said. “You all better be glad no one is on site or we all would be going to jail.”

“And I’m sure your daddy would have bailed us out,” Nicole said while looking at him. “Now, are you going to tell Zuri what happened?”

“Can I at least get some tissue?”

“Not until you explain what happened.”

Her eyes were filled with tears as she looked at us.

“Malcolm asked me to help him on a plan to get rid of you. He talked about an incident that happened awhile back and he was out for revenge. He figured since I was upset about your job that I would be willing to help.”

Nicole shook her head. “You sold your soul to the devil.”

“I only did it because the job was rightfully mine.”

“You did it because you were selfish and petty,” I said.

I looked at Tyrik who looked shocked. I don’t know why, but I guess he thought she wouldn’t be capable of doing this.

“Don’t act like you didn’t know about this,” Nicole said.

"I really didn't. My dad doesn't tell me a lot of things. Besides, you think he would have if he thought I would have gone to you about it?"

"He does have a point," Nicole said.

"What did you put in my drink, Erin?"

"Your drink was roofied. My cousin is a street pharmacist so I pretty much knew what dosage for you to have a bit of a memory lost."

"Street pharmacist. Funny," Nicole said.

"But I'm just now regaining my memory? How is that possible?"

"I can't answer that. Now, can I please leave? I think my nose is broken."

"Not until you answer one last question. Did Malcolm know all along that I was involved with Damon?"

"Why do you want to know that?"

"Because I need to know."

"Yes, he did. Can I go now?"

"One more thing. You're going to let myself, Damon, Nicole, and Chandler into this party."

"Why should I? For you all to destroy it?"

"No, for starters, we still need answers. A lot is going on and it seems as if Malcolm is in the center of it all."

"Are you trying to say my dad has been targeting you because of Damon?" Tyrik asked.

"Damon does work for Milo. He'll do anything to stay ahead of the game."

“And another thing, if you don’t let us in, I will go to the police and have you arrested for assault and harassment.”

“How are you going to do that?”

I pulled out my phone and pressed play on my memos app. Her confession was being played.

"Wow."

“Why are you so shocked? You thought I was going to hear you confess without recording it? Try me again and you will be going to jail.”

After giving her that bit of news, she agreed to put us on the guest list. After that, I told her she could leave. She was dripping blood everywhere as she walked out. I studied Tyrik, who sat down in a seat near the table. I wondered if the shock routine was really an act, but as he looked at me, he clearly wasn’t.

“You have to believe me when I say I didn’t know any of this.”

“I see that now, but what I don’t get is why did you act so cold towards me after the video was leaked?”

“I guess I couldn’t handle it. My dad was pressuring me to end things with you, which now I know why. But it was more of my pride than anything else.”

“You belittled me in front of a lot of people. You put the blame on me when you had a part in making it too.”

“Which I regret. Zuri, I never meant to hurt you, but I also had a reputation to uphold because of my dad. I know I shouldn’t have done it, and for that, I’m sorry.”

“Thank you,” I said softly.

He nodded and got up. “I think we can call it a day.”

“Yeah, we had enough excitement,” Nicole said.

“You both can go. I need to lock up.”

“Okay, but one more thing,” I said.

“What?”

“I need access to your father’s files.”

Damon

I laid in my hospital bed bored as hell since I couldn't do anything. I was ready to get back out there and finish this case so I can be done with the entire thing. Regardless of me being laid up, I wasn't going to stop working. There were other ways for me to get the information I needed. With Chandler digging up info, I'll be one step ahead of Malcolm and Milo.

The door slowly opened and my uncle walked in, giving me a wide grin.

"How's my favorite nephew doing?"

"I'm your only nephew," I said.

He sat beside me and started to watch TV. He glanced at me and noticed the stoic look I had.

"Besides being here, what's wrong?"

"You need to be honest with me, unc."

"What do you mean? I've always been honest with you."

"No, you haven't. Why have you never told me about the truck that pushed my dad off the road? Or the potassium chloride that was found in Escobar's system. Why did you cover up my parents' deaths?"

"Where did you get that information from?"

"That's not any of your concern. You tell me what your motive was for covering for Milo?"

"Do you really want to know? It will only bring up old skeletons that don't need to be dug up."

"These are my parents, unc. Your brother! I didn't have them growing up, but that doesn't mean I don't want justice for them. You're a part of what happened, so I have to know."

Julian sat there for a couple of minutes, not saying a word. I was starting to become impatient, when he looked at me.

"Just know that your parents loved you so much, Damon. I know they would be proud of the man that you have become. With what I told you, some of it was true, while some I had to lie about. It wasn't because I didn't trust you, it was because I had to. As you know, your parents' marriage was in shambles. Between their jobs, you, and their differences in opinions, they were finding other ways to cope with it all. For your mom, she chose to be with Milo, which was a huge mistake. The affair was going on for a year when your dad found out. When he did, he was livid, but he was more concerned than anything. He knew how dangerous Milo could be. Even your mom knew, but for some reason, she didn't care. She loved the thrill of being with him, which caused even more issues. Once your dad knew the truth, he put a plan into motion to get rid of Milo. He even asked me to help, which I did since I would do anything for my brother. But one thing that we should have remembered was that Milo was always one step ahead of everything."

"So he knew about the plan?"

Julian nodded. "He knew that your dad wasn't going to do anymore of his dirty work, so he planned an evening with some of the lords in the area, including Escobar. He poisoned his drink so he could kill him without anyone even knowing."

"But how did my dad end up shooting him?"

"As I mentioned before, an argument escalated, causing him to shoot him."

"So you're saying my mom knew what was going on?"

“About Escobar, yes, she did.”

“Wow.”

“As for the SUV, that was meant for Milo. Our plan was for him to use that car, he would lose control, and crash. Instead, your mom got into the car and your dad tried to stop her.”

“Wait, what?”

Julian took a deep breath and sighed. “I was the one who rigged the SUV. After your dad told me what he was planning, we mapped out a way for me to go into Milo’s place so I could rig the car. Unfortunately, the plan backfired. When your mom tried to leave, your dad followed her and she took the nearest car that was available. Of course she didn’t know what was going on, but your dad did.”

“So he tried to stop her.”

“Little did either of them know, there was another car that was following them. They tailgated the SUV, hitting it multiple times, causing it to go off the cliff.”

“So the person driving the car was the one who killed them?”

“Technically, I did, since the report came back as the cause being engine failure.”

“But someone pushed them off the road.”

“Yes, which the other car was explained in the actual accident report. There were two at the station, Damon. The one that was hacked, which I’m sure Chandler did, and the real accident report, which I had to destroy.”

"He found out about the SUV, didn’t he?”

“He did, but there was something else, Damon.”

"What?"

Julian sighed. "Milo is your real father."

I looked at Julian, not sure if he was telling the truth. I continued to stare while Julian got up.

"You're lying. Milo isn't my dad. My dad is Austin Baxter. Milo is some fucking lowlife who loves to destroy people."

"He's your father, Damon. That's the real reason why Austin wanted to go along with the plan. He was lied to about the fact that your mom had an affair and then Milo got her pregnant. That would make anyone go crazy."

"That still doesn't explain how you were involved."

"When he found out about the incident, he was ready to turn me into the police. There were a couple of things he was willing to do in order for me not to go to jail. One was the cover-up, and two was to take you in. He also wanted you to get into the business, which was accomplished with me putting you on this case."

"There's another reason, isn't it?"

"I would have to disregard any crime that he has been doing. That's why I pulled you out the first time because I knew he would never pay for the violence he ensured."

"Unbelievable," I whispered. "He knows, doesn't he?"

"He does. In fact, he was going to raise you, but I wasn't going to allow that. I didn't want you to grow up in that type of environment, so that was when the exchange was made. I covered up his crimes, not only for my part in the accident, but also to protect you."

"That's why you didn't want me to take any case involving Milo."

"No, but you're stubborn. That was the reason, along with I knew you would eventually want to start looking into your parents' deaths."

"I knew something was up when he recruited me."

"I really didn't want you to find out this way."

"I had to eventually. That doesn't change who I am though. You will always be my uncle."

He nodded. "Just like you will always be my nephew. That won't change."

"So now that I know the truth, shouldn't we try to stop Milo?"

"We will, but honestly after what happened, I don't want you on this case."

"Come on unc, I have been shot plenty of times."

"Yes, but now, there is more at stake. You have Milo and Malcolm. It's too much, Damon."

"I have dealt with much worse. Besides, Malcolm is not a factor."

"Oh really. He had someone shoot you."

"Because I threatened him."

The door opened and Zuri walked in with two brown bags. She nodded to Julian who did the same."

"What's in the bag?" I asked.

"Just the best barbecue ribs you'll ever experience in your life. I had to go to Duke's while I was here. I was safe Julian. My bodyguards were by my side the entire time."

"Glad to hear that."

"So how did it go?" I asked.

"Erin confessed. She was the one who did everything that night."

"Damn," I replied.

"In exchange for me not going to the police, I asked her to put our names on the guest list. That is, if you can go."

"Even though I might be released soon, you know I have to be on bed rest for two weeks. The party is this weekend."

"I know, but I was hoping that the chief would look the other way and possibly let you out for a few hours."

"Zuri—" Julian said.

"That's just enough time to get what we need and leave. He'll be back here or at the hotel before you know it."

"What if he injures himself even more? That's not a risk anyone should take."

"And we won't, right D?"

I looked from Julian to Zuri, knowing I should.

"Z, maybe it's best if I rest."

Before I could say anything more, Zuri's new burner phone started to ring. We change out phones pretty often, so only us, Nicole, and Chandler have each other's numbers in case we need them.

She picked up the phone and smiled. "Hey Nicole, what's up?"

Even I could hear the screams on the other end as I sat up.

"Nicole, calm down and tell me what's wrong."

I looked at Julian who leaned in closer to Zuri.

"Oh no! Where are you, sweetie? At the hotel? I'm coming."

She hung up and looked at the two of us with tears in her eyes. She was slowly falling when Julian got up to steady her.

"Baby, what's going on?"

She tried to talk, but she started to hyperventilate.

"Okay, sweetie, calm down," Julian said as he tried to find something for Zuri to breath into. He found a small bag and told her to take deep breaths.

"It's Chandler, isn't it?" I softly said.

"He's dead, Damon."

I looked away, trying to come to grips with what she just said. How could he be dead when I just saw him?

"Did Nicole say what happened?" Julian asked.

Zuri nodded. "She was coming back to the room when she saw him lying on the floor. He was shot in the head."

"Where the hell was security?" Julian yelled. He jumped up and grabbed his phone.

"Let me see what happened. What about his parents? Were they there?"

"I don't know."

He excused himself and went out to the hall to talk. I was still staring at the window when Zuri put her arms around me.

"I'm so sorry, baby," she whispered before kissing the top of my head. I didn't even acknowledge her as the news slowly sunk in. My best friend since kindergarten was murdered, and it was all my fault.

Zuri

I watched Damon as he was staring into space. He hasn't spoken since he found out about Chandler, which was tearing me apart. Those two were like brothers, so I knew this was hard on him.

I wanted to see Nicole, but Julian advised me not to. Until he was able to find out what actually happened, he wanted me to stay with Damon. Since Julian is out of his jurisdiction, he couldn't be a part of the investigation, but could find out what happened to the officers that were supposedly on duty when it happened.

"I don't understand. Where were the cops Julian hired? Why did they let this happen?"

"It wasn't the cops, it was me."

I looked at Damon who was still staring into space. I went over to him, wondering what he meant.

"What?"

"This is my fault. If I didn't ask him to hack into the police's flies, none of this would have happened."

"You don't know that. There is so much going on that no one knows who is being targeted. You saw what happened to you."

"Yeah, and you too. No matter who I'm associated with, everyone is in danger."

"Baby, look at me."

He wouldn't, which made me push his face towards mine.

"Look at me. None of this is your fault. We are all dealing with two sick individuals who want power and they'll destroy anyone for it. Chandler was always loyal to you, so you know he wouldn't blame you either."

"I know, but—"

"No, Damon. Stop. All we can do now is get justice for his murder. We know that either Milo or Malcolm had something to do with it, so we have to find a way to get rid of them once and for all."

"I know this is Milo. Julian told me some things about my parents' deaths. Milo is my father."

"What did you say?"

Damon went on to explain that the affair was longer than Julian claimed and that he was the one who rigged the SUV. He even went into the exchange Julian made with Milo for him to raise him. To me, that was pretty noble to sacrifice so much to raise a child that wasn't even his blood.

"I think that's brave for Julian to do."

"It is. He didn't have to do it, but he did. I just hope it doesn't come back to haunt him."

"I'll go to that party. I need to see if Malcolm has anything to do with this."

"It's Milo who—"

"No, for some reason, I don't think those two have been honest. I think they're still in alliance with each other."

Damon looked at me as I sat beside him.

"Remember the incident that I told you about when Malcolm shot that guy? Milo was one of the men there. I really think those two have been in cahoots with each other the entire time, but trying to throw everyone off by saying they hate each other. That's why whoever is targeted would put the blame on the other."

"Or throw them off so one of them can put a plan into action."

"Exactly."

"You're not doing this alone."

"But you said—"

"That was before my best friend was killed. Now, I'm going to do what I can to make sure those bastards get what they deserve."

I nodded, wondering what Damon had planned. I got my burner phone again to call my parents. I had to know if they were okay.

Damon

A couple of days have passed and it was the night of Malcolm's party. After spending two more days in the hospital, Dr. Westbourne said I could be released, but only on the condition that I remain on bed rest for two weeks. That wasn't going to happen. I already told Julian I would be attending the party, which he hated, but figured if anything happened it would be entirely on me. That I can agree on.

He did confirm that Chandler's murder was either done by Milo or Malcolm. Their street stigma was written in his blood in the bathroom and near the window. We all know it was a message saying they were on to us and they would kill whoever was in their way.

I was in the hotel room, putting on my tie, when Zuri walked out of the bathroom. She looked beautiful dressed in a navy blue backless gown. Her hair was pinned up, making her look even sexier, which I didn't think was even possible.

"Wow, Z, you look stunning."

"You look pretty handsome yourself. I finally get to see you in a suit," she said as she came to me. She began fixing my tie, getting it right, which I had a hard time doing.

"I watched my dad do his all of the time."

"I'm glad your parents are fine."

She smiled. "Me too. They're having fun out there. At least someone is. I didn't tell them about Chandler though."

"It's best if you didn't. You don't need to worry them."

"I think this was a way for them to reconnect, so at least this worked out for them."

"That's good."

"Did Julian ever mention the cops who supposedly were watching Chandler and Nicole? What happened to them that day?"

"They were knocked out and taken to the back of the hotel, that's why Nicole didn't see them."

"This is horrible. I feel so bad for her and his parents."

"Yeah, they're devastated. They wanted to take his body back to Houston so they could plan the funeral, but that's not going to happen. He has to stay here for an autopsy, which they still haven't done."

"Did Julian give them more protection? I really don't want anything to happen to them."

"He has, but even if they try to leave, they can't. Julian suggested they should wait to do anything until all of this blows over. Knowing those two, they'd try to do something at the funeral."

"That's shitty if they did."

"Nothing surprises me anymore with them. But they're not going back to the city."

"I kind of figured. Where are they heading?"

"Julian didn't even tell me, so I'm not sure."

She sighed. "I just pray they'll be okay."

"Me too. If they didn't come here, none of this would have happened."

"Maybe not, but I think to some extent, Nicole and Chandler wanted to take the risk and come. Even though they had protection, there could still be issues along the way. I'm just glad I was able to spend the time I did with him. I'm going to miss him."

Zuri gave me a hug as I took deep breaths. Hopefully all of this blows over soon so he can have the proper memorial that he deserves.

We pulled apart and I picked up my suit jacket and gun.

"You ready?"

She nodded. "Yeah, let's take down these bastards."

She put her hand into a fist and we gave each other dab. That's when I knew she was ready for anything.

"Let's do this."

I was heading to the door when I felt a sharp pain near my wound. Zuri gave a concerned look as I held out my hand.

"I'm good, baby. Let's go."

She slowly nodded and took my hand and went to the door.

***

The drive to the venue was an awkward one as we were in silence the entire ride. I think the two of us were sort of nervous about how things would play out. I slowly put my hand on Zuri's thigh as she looked at me before going back to the road.

"With everything going on, I haven't told you that I asked Tyrik to go into Malcolm's files."

I looked at her as if she was crazy. "You did what?"

"I asked him a couple of days ago to look up his files. He didn't know what was going on that night or even now, so he's safe."

I shook my head, realizing she was being naïve. No one is safe or innocent. At this point, everyone, especially Tyrik, wasn't to be trusted.

"How do you know he didn't tell his dad? We could be going into a trap."

"I promise you, he was just as disgusted as I was about what happened, that's why he wants to help."

"How convenient. Where was this attitude at when you needed him the most? Oh, I forgot, he was calling you a slut and a whore then."

"That's not fair, Damon."

"How can you be so trusting towards him?"

"Have you ever felt that way about someone where your instincts are telling you that you should trust them? That's how I feel about Tyrik. I really think he'll come through."

"I'm sorry, but I don't trust him."

"Which I understand, but regardless, he's going to have info regarding his dad and possibly yours."

I cringed when she said that. That man will never be my father.

We approached the venue, seeing how pack it was as guests were waiting outside to get in. Zuri told Erin to put us on the VIP list, so we didn't have to wait.

Once we were confirmed, we walked in, taking in everything as Zuri looked around.

"I could have done this so much better."

"Are you worried about that now?"

"She stole my job, so there's still some animosity."

I glanced over and saw Tyrik looking at Zuri. I don't trust his ass one bit. He walked over near the bar and motioned for us to come with him. Zuri walked off, leaving me standing in the middle of the room.

"Are you coming or are you going to stand there looking like an ass?"

I sighed and followed her. We got to the end of the hall when Tyrik stopped us.

"Before I say anything, I have to know are you going to run and tell Milo?"

"I know you don't trust me, just like I don't trust you. but Zuri does, so I have to take it for what it's worth."

"I know you're a cop. Zuri told me."

I stared at her while she looked at Tyrik.

"Trust me, I'm not going to say anything. My dad has done a lot of things, so I want justice too. Also, I heard about Nicole's husband. Please accept my condolences."

"Which your dad had something to do with," I chided.

"I have no doubt he did. Milo did too, which I wanted to tell you two. They have been working together, even when they had their supposed turf war. They have been in alliance for years, but only did this to throw their enemies off."

"Is there a reason why they're doing this?" Zuri asked.

Tyrik stared at me and sighed. "It looks like the two are brothers, adoptive brothers to be exact. I've done some digging, and even tried to talk to a few people, but no one wanted to cooperate except for one person, my great grandmother, Estelle. She told me everything."

"So why didn't you ever realize this?" I asked.

"Because we never associated with her. Now, I know why."

"This shit gets more fucked up every second," I said.

"So, I guess this means we're cousins, in a way."

I looked at Zuri and she shrugged.

"She didn't tell me. That was something else Estelle told me. That woman knows everything."

"I see."

"Listen, you probably think I'm a bad guy, especially with how I treated Zuri, but I assure you that I'm not. My dad basically blocked me out of a lot of things and treated me as if I didn't exist, so I want him to be punished just like you do. Milo too; I never liked him."

"I guess we have that in common."

"You probably will never trust me and that's fine. Just know that I am on the same team."

Zuri looked at me and nodded.

I stared at him, not knowing if I should really trust him. This could be a damn trap that could prove deadly.

"There is one thing I did find out about this venue. This is not the first time my dad used it. In fact, this is sort of his hideaway that he stores a lot of personal files at. You can go take a look for yourself and find anything that you think could be beneficial to use against him."

"How do I know you're not saying this so you can be alone with Zuri?"

Tyrik sighed. "What Z and I had was just a replacement for what she had with you. I was never in the same league with you. She wanted you all along, man. I was just a substitute."

I continued to stare at him as he looked at me. "Where's the room?"

"Upstairs and three doors to your right," he said while handing me a key.

"This will get you in. I had to pickpocket it from my dad. He doesn't leave anywhere without it."

"Why did you never mention that your dad owned this place?" Zuri asked.

"Because you never asked. I have to go back to the party, but you two can go up there and look."

"I still feel like this is a trap."

"It's not, Damon."

"It better not be. If it is, I'll be back to find you and put a bullet in you."

"Like you were going to do anyway? I know about the hit out on me and my dad. You better hope yours doesn't find out that you're talking to me."

"If he does, I have a bullet with his name on it too. Just hope that this shit is legit," I said as I took Zuri's hand. She looked at Tyrik and mouthed thank you before we headed upstairs.

Before going any further, Zuri grabbed my arm and looked at me.

"Not everyone is bad, baby. Yes, he was an ass with what happened, but he's legit."

I nodded, not knowing what more to say about it. We went up the stairs and to the room that Tyrik instructed. I used the key to open it, we walked inside and I closed the door. Zuri was about to turn on the light, when I stopped her.

"Don't. That'll bring unwanted attention," I said and threw a pocket flashlight to her.

"You conveniently had this?"

"I'm a cop, baby. I'm always prepared."

She gave a sexy smile and I shook my head.

"Don't do that now."

"Do what?"

"Turn me the hell on."

"You can't do anything about it."

"You want to bet on that? I'll have you bent over on that desk so quick you wouldn't know what hit you."

"And you'll injure yourself again."

"It'll be worth it, especially when I make you cum."

She shivered and smiled. "We're getting off track right now. We have to find what we're looking for before someone comes in here."

"No one should since this is a secret room."

Zuri bent down to look around the desk while I grabbed another flashlight from my pocket and started searching throughout the room. I was about to look behind the bookshelf when I heard footsteps approaching. Zuri looked at me and I quickly told her to hide. As soon as I was about to find a spot, the door opened and someone walked in. The light quickly came on as I turned to face the person.

"Erin."

"Damon, what are you doing in here?"

I had to think of a lie quick, but I was more concerned about where Zuri hid. I looked to my side and saw her peeking from underneath the desk. She rolled her eyes at the mention of Erin.

"I was looking for the restroom and surprisingly, this is not it."

"No it's not. How did you get in here?"

"It was unlocked."

"That's impossible. This room is always locked," she said while rushing in. She quickly looked around as I glanced at her.

"Is it something you're looking for?"

"That's none of your business."

"I was just wondering since you're looking all around the room."

"The restroom is downstairs near the ballroom," she said while going to the door. She was waiting on me to leave, which I didn't want to since Zuri was still there. She looked near the desk, as I was praying that she wouldn't look down.

"You know, I'm glad I ran into you, Damon. There's something I need to talk to you about."

"Why do you need to talk to me?"

"There are some things that you need to know about Zuri."

"I know about your little run-in. I see your face is slowly healing."

She gave me an irritated look before coming over to me. She slowly touched my shoulder while trying to give me a seductive look, which wasn't attractive at all.

"Thank your thuggish girlfriend for that. I look like I was beaten."

"You were."

She smirked while looking at the desk again. I don't know why, but I had a feeling she knew Zuri was under there.

"Has Zuri ever told you about when she first arrived to L.A? How nervous and scared she was to move to a new city."

"Why is that news? Anyone would feel that way."

"That's true, but her story was a little different. You see, Zuri had a secret that no one knew about until she was forced to tell it to me when I saw her puking in the bathroom one morning. Did you know that she was pregnant?"

"Yes, Zuri told me."

"But did she tell you the entire story?"

"Yes, she did. What are you trying to say, Erin?"

"Oh, so she told you she had an abortion? Wow, I wouldn't have thought a man of your caliber would be okay with that."

I tilted my head, wondering what the hell she was talking about.

"What? Zuri had a miscarriage. She didn't have an abortion."

Erin laughed. "Wow, she is something else. The fact that she lied about even being pregnant, but she had the nerve to lie and say she miscarried is just plain wrong."

"What are you trying to prove here? You're mad because she busted your damn face so you want revenge."

"I'm trying to tell you who the real Zuri Caldwell is. She's a liar and a snake who would do anything to get what she wants. She chose her career over you and your child. That should tell you how much she cared about you."

"You're lying."

Erin smiled. "Sorry to disappoint you, but I'm not. I'm the one who took her to the clinic and took care of her after the procedure. You should ask her."

She turned on her heels and walked to the door. She turned around and smiled.

"Oh yeah, and give me the key that Tyrik graciously gave you. He's such a traitor."

I went up to her and stared into her eyes. I looked at Zuri, who wouldn't even look at me. Tears were streaming down her cheeks as she tried not to make a sound. I looked back at Erin and pushed her back into the room. Zuri got up from underneath the desk and ran to the hall. Before Erin could say anything, I locked the door and threw the key down the stairs. Hopefully no one will find her.

I tried to catch up to Zuri who was speed walking to the stairs. She almost tripped on her gown as I caught up with her. I pulled her to me so she could look at me.

"Let me go, Damon."

"That's the other secret you've been keeping? Why didn't you tell me?"

"Why would I? You would have never forgiven me for it."

"I'm not going to lie, it hurts like hell that you didn't tell me. The fact that you went and made a decision about *our* child on your own. How could you do that?"

"I'm so sorry, Damon. I was going to tell you, but—"

"But when, Zuri? That's something you should have told me when we first reconnected. I had to hear that from Erin and she only did it to get back at you."

"I don't know what else to say. At the time, I thought it was the best decision. I was starting my career and learning you were a hit man. That was not an environment to raise a child."

"We could have made it work, Zuri. Now, I guess we won't know that, now will we?"

I walked past her and headed to the stairs. She yelled out my name, but I ignored her. Although I shouldn't have left her there, I couldn't be around her right now.

Zuri

I watched as Damon went down the stairs, which literally tore me apart. Nicole warned me that this would happen. I should have been honest with him from the start, but of course, I didn't listen.

I clutched my stomach, feeling the pain within me as I steadied myself on the wall. I took deep breaths as I felt someone approach me.

"Damon."

"No, it's Tyrik. What happened?" he asked as he came up to me.

"He left."

"What? Why did he do that?"

"Because he knows about the abortion."

Tyrik sighed. "Oh."

"That bitch told him while she caught him in the room. I think she knew I was hiding underneath the desk and spilled everything."

"Wow. I'm really sorry. Trust me, her ass is gone after tonight anyway. She fucked up with the food order and the DJ, so I know my dad will be pissed."

"I really don't care," I mumbled.

"Zuri, I know that was horrible what happened, but you knew he would find out eventually. You brought this on yourself."

"Wow, thank you for your encouragement."

"I wasn't going to sugar coat anything, if that's what you wanted to hear. We're human, so we're going to make fucked up mistakes. It's part of our nature to."

"So I should go find him and make things right, huh?"

"You think?"

I shook my head at Tyrik and he smiled.

"I never thought I would be talking to you about the man I'm with."

"Well, things change. People change."

"That's so true."

"I want you to be happy, Z. Like I said to Damon, he was always the real deal for you. I was just a stand in."

"We did have some moments together."

"We always had fun, that was no doubt, but I knew where your heart was. I had to do what was necessary for you to see that."

"What?"

"You think I wanted to say those things to you? Like I said before, my father was pressuring me to end things with you. But I didn't do it because of him, I did it so you could move on and be with the man you wanted. You were just scared to be with him."

"Do you blame me? I had only known him for six months at the time and I was already pregnant by him. I didn't know what to do."

"But you do now. You know you want to be with him, so find a way to get back with him. If you have to beg, deep throat him, whatever, do it."

I laughed. "Did you seriously just say that?"

"Hell, that would get me back."

"Whatever, Tyrik."

He smiled. "But seriously, try to find a way to win him back. That's the only way. Besides, he's crazy about you, he just needs time to process everything."

I nodded. "I know. But have you moved on from the engagement?"

"Why are you worried about me?"

"I had to ask."

He nodded. "I did, actually. You remember Christette?"

"Yeah, she works in accounting."

He smiled. "Let's just say she helped me through that period."

I smirked. "I'm sure she did."

"I really like her, Zuri."

"I'm glad you do."

He came over to me and gave me a hug. I slowly put my arms around him, wondering if I should. Although Tyrik just confessed to being with another woman, this moment felt a bit awkward.

"Look at this. Fucking traitor."

We slowly looked over and saw two men dressed in black suits staring at the two of us. Tyrik stood in front of me and sighed.

"What the hell do you both want?"

One of them pulled out a .45 and aimed it at Tyrik. "We have orders to kill you, along with her behind you."

I looked from the men to Tyrik, wondering what the hell was going on. Unless…

"Who gave you that order?"

The other guy aimed his gun at us and smiled. "Your own father."

"Erin must have told him what you did," I whispered.

"He wouldn't do this. I'm his son."

"Like he gives a shit," one of the guys said. He was about to shoot Tyrik when a shot rang out. The bullet hit him in the shoulder, as another went to his temple. We ducked as the other guy tried to shoot us, but instead, got himself in the chest. I turned around and saw Damon coming near us, holding his gun at the two men on the ground. Blood was seeping through the beige carpet as he looked at us.

"Are you two okay?"

"Yeah. How did you know we were here?"

"I was coming back up to talk to you, but saw this instead."

Damn, thank you," Tyrik said.

"No problem. We better go before someone else comes up here."

He let me walk first as we were about to go down the stairs, but stopped when we saw Malcolm walking up.

"Well, well, well, if it isn't my no good ass son."

"Dad, just leave them alone. If you have a problem with me, then so be it."

"Oh, I have a problem with you alright. You went behind my damn back and were trying to expose me. Your own damn father!"

"You have done nothing but manipulate and terrorize people for years. It's time that something is done about it."

"Something will be done about it. It'll be your ass out of my damn life."

He pulled out a revolver and shot him right in the chest. I screamed as Tyrik fell to the floor as Malcolm kept shooting him. Damon tried to take a shot, but when he started firing at us, he grabbed my hand and led me down the hall.

"You can't run muthafuckers! I'll find you eventually!"

I looked behind me as I watched Tyrik on the ground, helpless. I wanted to help him, but I knew I couldn't.

"We have to call 911," I said to Damon.

"We will, but right now, we need to get the hell out of here."

We found a fire escape near the end of the hall as Damon used his foot to kick the window out. I ducked as the glass shattered everywhere. He leaned down and I could tell his wound was bothering him. He looked at me and motioned for me to go.

I looked down and saw how steep the landing was and stared at him.

"I'm wearing a dress."

"Is that a major concern right now? Go!"

I sighed and went to the stoop. I grabbed the ladder and carefully went down, hoping my gown didn't get in the way as I continued. I looked up to see Damon slowly trying to come down as well. My gown got caught on one of the steps, making me wobble on the stairs. I tried to get the fabric off from the ladder, but couldn't.

"My dress caught!"

"Rip it!"

I was finally able to get it off as I pulled it from the step and it flew down. I continued going to the bottom as Damon made his way down.

“There’re probably some guys waiting for us. We might have to split up.”

“I’m not splitting up.”

“Z—”

“Stop, Damon! Despite what just happened, we’re going to do this together. Are you with me?”

He sighed, grabbed my hand, and we headed to the car. Hopefully no one was around to follow us.

Damon

Once we made our getaway, I was surprised that no one was trying to follow us. I looked at Zuri. Besides calling 911 in regards to Tyrik, she hasn't said much since we left.

"Zuri."

She slowly turned to stare at me. "What are we going to do?"

I didn't look at her as I continued to drive. "Everything will be okay."

"That's not reassuring when there are men with guns trying to kill us."

"I promise you we'll get through this."

"What about you? You're doing too much. And Tyrik? I don't even know if he's okay."

"I have to admit, he was legit going to bat for us, so I hope he pulls through."

She looked away as I knew she was crying. I put my hand on her thigh and she turned to stare.

"We're going to find a way out of this. As long as we got each other's backs, then nothing will go wrong. Am I right?"

"You're right, but—"

"We'll talk about that later, Z. Right now, we need to get rid of these sick fucks. Also, you need to check on your parents."

"I sent them a text. They're okay."

"I really think you need to hear their voices, just in case anything is up."

She nodded and reached for her phone. I fled down the highway, which was surprising. Maybe God was watching over us as I exited off and went to our destination. I already gave Julian a heads up, so he told us not to go to the hotel, but to an area that he instructed. Zuri put the phone down and sighed. "Neither are answering their phones."

I took a deep breath while I pulled into the car port and looked to see if Julian was there. I received a message letting me know to come inside. Zuri stared at me as we slowly got out of the car. I think she was thinking the same as I was. Something wasn't right.

"You think something is up?"

"There's only one way to find out," I said as I got out. I reached under my seat for my extra gun. I handed it to Zuri who sighed.

"You're going to have to use it."

She nodded as I got out. I waited for her to do the same as we slowly approached the door. I knocked while I motioned for her to aim her gun at whoever answers it. We have to prepare ourselves if it is a trap. The door slowly opened and it was my uncle, who gave us a surprised look.

"What the hell are you two doing?"

"You can never be too careful, right?" I said while walking inside. Zuri put her gun down and followed Julian, who closed the door and stared at us.

"How did you know to come here?"

Julian shrugged. "I just found the place and saw that it was abandoned. No one should find you two here."

I gave a stern look while going to the wall. Julian gave a concerned look of his own, wondering what was going on.

“How’s Nicole and Chandler's parents? You never mentioned where they were headed.”

“I figured it was best since their last visit was disastrous.”

“Which I’m still trying to wrap my head around. I mean, you said they were all safe and that they weren’t to be seen in public, yet you allowed Chandler and Nicole to freely be around town. Why is that?”

“Because they had security at the time.”

“Yes, but not when Chandler was murdered. Conveniently, you told Alan and Nigel to take the day off.”

Zuri looked confused as I went over to my uncle.

“What are you talking about, Damon?”

“I did a little digging of my own after Chandler passed because I knew something wasn’t right with that. Not only did Detective Ramirez inform me of those two being off, but he also mentioned that you went by Chandler’s room that day. Why didn’t you mention that?”

“I went by there to see if everything was okay.”

“Yet, you did so when Nicole was conveniently with Zuri, am I right?”

“What are you getting at?”

“Did you have something to do with Chandler’s murder?”

Julian laughed. “Why would you think that? I considered Chandler a part of the family.”

"Cut the bullshit! I got Ramirez to go over your damn head to obtain security footage at the hotel. Turns out not only were you there, but also Fatone and Salley. What the hell did you do, Julian?"

"I didn't do anything!"

"Stop lying!" I exclaimed while I put my gun to his temple. He let out a huge breath while I clicked the trigger. "Tell me why I shouldn't blow your brains out right now?"

"Damon, please!" Zuri yelled.

I stared at Julian, my finger still on the trigger as I felt the cold steel go to my temple. I closed my eyes as I didn't move. Zuri pulled out her gun and aimed it as well.

"We meet again, Damon."

"How did you know where to find us, Malcolm?"

"Because I'm the one who set this up. You see, your trusty uncle has been working for us for years, am I right, Julian?"

"Put down the gun, Malcolm!" Zuri yelled.

My eyes went to my uncle, who had his head down. "Yeah, unc, I want to know all about you working with Malcolm and Milo."

"It's not what you think."

"I'm sure, even though you killed Chandler."

"I had no choice! He knew too much!"

"Stop talking, Julian!" Malcolm demanded.

I pressed the steel even harder on Julian as Zuri had hers on Malcolm. Someone was going to die in this damn warehouse today.

"Someone better talk or I'll shoot," I said.

Julian sighed. “He knew that I was embezzling money from the police department. He also knew I took money from Malcolm and Milo.”

“Why? You were doing enough already with them.”

“To cover a few gambling debts. I had to do it. If I didn’t, I would have been killed.”

“You still might be!”

“You won’t kill your uncle, would you? Remember, he’s the only family you have,” Malcolm taunted.

“Shut the fuck up!”

“Or what? You want another bullet in that wound of yours? Should have killed your ass in that parking lot.”

“You have the opportunity now, so finish it off.”

“Oh my God!” Zuri exclaimed.

“Look at Zuri. You saw your ex shot and now your man is about to be killed. This hasn’t been your best day, has it?”

I stared at Zuri as she looked at Malcolm.

“If you even try to shoot me, I’ll have an army of men in here. Do you want that?”

“Do it, Zuri.”

“I suggest you don’t, especially if you want to know where your friend is.”

Zuri’s hands were shaking at the mention of Nicole. I should have known something was wrong when Julian wouldn’t reveal her whereabouts.

"That's right, I have your friend and Chandler's parents all locked away with your parents, Zuri. I'm sure they're all having a good old time together."

"You bitch," she whispered as she put the gun down.

"Technically, we wouldn't need you for that since Julian knows where they are, don't you? Is Milo there too?"

I motioned for Zuri to come to Julian while I went to Malcolm. Before he could attempt to flee, I grabbed him by his wrists and pulled them back, causing him to laugh.

"Listen here, muthafucker. I'm not in the mood for games. Either you cooperate or I don't have a problem shooting you between your eyes. So start talking!"

He spit in my face so I had his wrist in one hand and went in my pocket with the other to grab my handcuffs. I slapped them on him and threw him to the ground. I would shoot him, but I want him to rot in prison.

The door busted open as L.A.P.D. came through the doors. I shoved Malcolm over to one of the officers as someone came to me.

"Detective Baxter, I'm Sergeant Jones," he said while extending his hand. I gave him a handshake and nodded.

"Thank you for the heads up with O'Neal. We have been trying to get him for years, but never had evidence that would actually stick."

"I wonder why," I said while staring at Julian.

"Do you want to press charges on O'Neal?"

I glanced at Malcolm while he gave a slide smile.

"Yes. I hope you throw the damn book at him. As well as his partner," I said while staring at Julian.

"We will need for you to come in for your statement."

"I will, but my job is not done."

"Milo?"

"Yeah. Get O'Neal into questioning. He'll confess to taking six people hostage," I said as I took out my phone and hit share for the recording of him and Julian.

"I have an idea where they are, but I need confirmation."

"Certainly."

"I'll be back. Watch and see," Malcolm said.

"You won't be since you shot your own son. Get the hell out of here."

As Malcolm was being hauled away, another officer slapped cuffs on Julian as I stared at him. He looked at me with sad eyes.

"I never meant to hurt you."

"I'm sure. Instead, you sold your soul for money."

"Damon—"

"You will have a shitload of charges against you, including murder and accessory to kidnapping."

"Damon—"

"Where is everyone, Julian?"

"They're not in St. Croix."

"Tell me where they are!"

"They will kill me if I reveal that."

"I will kill you if you don't," I threatened as two officers grabbed a hold of me.

"They're at Milo's island near Belize. Zuri, your parents were at the resort, but Milo found out and had them kidnapped."

"Found out? More like you told him."

"That I didn't do, but with Nicole and Chandler's parents, I told him their whereabouts."

"There's an innocent child in this, Julian! You know Milo could give a shit about kids."

"That's why I didn't want to do it."

"But you still did. I want the information about that island."

"I don't know much."

I was close to pulling out my gun again when Zuri came over to him. She gave him a pleading look.

"Julian, please. So many lives are at stake. If you know anything, can you please share."

"Zuri, the only thing I know is that it's near Belize. It's on the outskirt by itself so no one could access it. There could be other compounds in the area, so I can't give an exact one."

"I know you've been there, so there has to be something that stood out."

Julian slowly nodded. "It was. There were two lion statues in the center, as well as a fountain."

"That's it?"

“That’s all.”

“Thanks. Now get him out of my face,” I demanded as he was read his rights and was hauled away. He turned around and mouthed “I’m sorry” before being pushed to the door.

While Sergeant Jones was asking me if I needed backup to go to Belize, I told him no. I figured I needed to do this on my own. Whether he’ll be in a Belize or American prison cell, Milo Regetta will be caught and serve.

Zuri

When the excitement was over and Julian and Malcolm were arrested, I was still in shock over what I learned. There were too many questions that I needed answers to, which were making me angry and anxious. I looked at Damon, who was shocked himself about everything. Honestly, I had my suspicions about Julian. He was always giving the runaround about certain things and wasn't around for certain periods of time. I also always found it strange that he would have different hideaways in various cities. Now, I knew why. Even though I had my reservations, I didn't want to tell Damon about them since Julian was his uncle.

We were back at the hotel, packing our things, when I looked at Damon. He was in a daze as he was putting his shirts in his carryall. I went over to him and held his hands.

"Talk to me. I know you're hurting."

He looked down at our hands and put mine to his lips to kiss them.

"There's so much that I learned today. From you and our baby, to my own uncle. Even Tyrik. I guess you really don't know a person like you thought."

I held his hands tighter as he looked to the window.

"Chandler didn't deserve to die. Even Tyrik didn't deserve what he got."

I wiped the tears from my cheeks as I sat down on the bed. "At least I was able to get some information about him. I just hope he pulls through."

"It's good that his mom still talks to you."

"At first, I thought it would be awkward, but she knew how concerned I was. She knew that Malcolm would eventually do this.

She even tried to warn Tyrik about having a relationship with him, but he wanted to know him. Have you heard anything about the jet?" I asked while getting up. Sergeant Jones lent Damon the department's private jet to take us to Belize. I didn't think that could be possible, but I'll do anything to get to my loved ones.

"They should be arriving soon. I'm just as anxious as you are."

"Would we need anything, as far as a passport or—"

He pulled out a bag from his carryall. "We got everything we need, so you don't have to worry about that."

"What if we don't get there in time? What if Malcolm warned Milo about what happened?"

"You can't think like that right now. You have to remain positive and pray that they're okay."

"How did all of this happen? Why are Milo and Malcolm messing with us?"

"Because they figured they can. But don't worry, this shit is going to be resolved soon. We lost too many people that we care about."

I nodded as he kissed my forehead. "I'm glad that you're with me."

Damon smiled. "I'm glad too. You're holding your own, but you still need to work on your timing. When I want you to shoot, you shoot."

"You know I'm still hesitant on a gun."

"You've been around them since you've met me."

I shrugged. "No one would be used to it if they haven't experienced one. But I still would like to know who the guy was that Malcolm shot."

"That I can answer. Sergeant Jones told me after I explained the story. Turns out it was Thomas Alvarez, a Belize diplomat. He was visiting both Malcolm and Milo when everything went down. He had funded their organization for years and it turned out a deal they had planned went south. Malcolm got pissed, an argument escalated, and he shot him."

"I can see who has the trigger finger between the two."

"Definitely. Baby, I never wanted any of this for you. Now your family and Nicole are involved and I feel disgusted by it."

"D, we talked about this. I would have been targeted regardless. As for you, you have lost your best friend and your uncle. We need to take back what we lost. Are you ready to?"

"Of course."

We sealed it with a fist bump when Damon's phone vibrated. He looked at it and nodded.

"It's time."

I nervously nodded. Hopefully things will go smoothly and our loved ones will return with us.

***

As the jet came and we were seated with the pilot, I stared at the blue skies, taking in how breathtaking the day looked. I would have enjoyed this day more if my family was safely with me. These past few days felt like a bad dream that I wish I could wake up from.

I looked at Damon who was looking up some places in Belize. I stared at the laptop and sighed.

"You're trying to find the place Julian was talking about?"

"Yeah. I was hoping there would be a picture online. No such luck."

"Did you really think he would have?"

“It was a long shot, but we need to have a plan when we land.”

“What will that be?”

“We have to find out exactly where they have everyone. We have to search every room, basement, tunnel, what have you.”

“And how’s that going to happen?”

“Leave that part to me.”

I leaned back in my seat and closed my eyes. “I just hope they’re okay.”

“We both do,” he said while taking my hand. He squeezed it and I put my head on his shoulder.

"I know this is probably the most awkward time to admit this, but I love you.”

I looked at him while he stared down at me. “You what?”

“Zuri, I’ve been in love with you from the first moment I saw you five years ago. You should have known that anyway when I was trying to convince you to stay with me.”

“Damon, so much has happened. Would you really want to be with me?”

“Yes, things are a little strained right now regarding our child, but we will make things work.”

“Why do I feel like this is the same talk we had five years ago.”

“Because you’re scared now, just like you were then too. Zuri, I never admitted to you because I felt you weren’t ready to hear it. I know you feel the same way, but you don’t want to say it. My feelings have always been known.”

"You loved me the first moment you saw me?"

"Yes, I did. I knew you were special and I didn't want to lose you."

I looked down as the tears began to fall. I'm usually not a crybaby. The last time I really cried was the day I walked out on Damon. But what he said really got to me. I never wanted to admit it, but he has always been the love of my life.

"I love you too."

He smiled. "I'm glad you're finally admitting it."

"Which was something we should have admitted."

"We're doing it now, so that's what matters."

He smiled as I pressed my lips against his. Although we just admitted our feelings, I was still feeling a little weary.

"Like I said, we'll get through that, Zuri. Don't worry about that."

I nodded and I closed my eyes, hoping that I could get some sleep.

Damon

Once I told Zuri that I loved her, I felt a burden being lifted from me. I have been waiting to admit that to her for a while now, but I always felt it wasn't the right time. I realized there will never be a good time, so I let go of any issues I had regarding it and went through with it.

We reached Belize in five hours as my anxiety kicked in. This was the moment we have been waiting for. To take down Milo and rescue our loved ones. This was going to be an effort that the two of us have to work on together, but I have no doubt that we will come out on top.

Since we still didn't know the exact location of Milo's compound, we had to find a place to strategize our next move. Sergeant Jones enlisted a friend of his in the area, Leo Campos, to help with this case. At first, I didn't want any help, but now it was good that there was someone who was willing to help. I just hope we can trust him.

We met with him at our landing spot. He immediately greeted us as we sat down.

"How did you enjoy the flight here?" he asked in a heavy accent.

"Very long," Zuri replied.

"I can imagine, but Eric wanted you both to arrive immediately. We were surprised you were able to come in a private jet, so I'm sure it was an experience."

"It definitely was," Zuri commented.

"We know all about Milo and his organized crime ring. Since he has a home here, he has done a couple of dealings. He even paid off some of our men to keep quiet about it."

"Typical," I mumbled.

"But weren't you undercover on his case for two years and you never knew about this place?"

"It's not like he was bragging about it. Besides, how did you know it was for two years?"

"I had to do my own research about you. No offense, but I do it for anyone from other parts of the country. You can't trust everyone nowadays."

"None taken."

"So it's your loved ones that are being held hostage?" Leo asked Zuri.

"Yes, and I'm wondering why we're not doing anything about it."

"I understand your frustration, but we have to strategize on how we're going to carry out their rescue. We can't just go in with our guns blazing, shooting up everything and everyone," Leo said.

"That sounds like an excellent plan," Zuri said.

"And you'll probably be the one shot or killed. Do you want that?" I asked.

"I just want to see them."

"And you will, but we need a plan. We can't go in blind."

"I agree," Leo said.

Since Leo knew about Milo's compound, we had an idea on the location. He mapped out the area for us, which was beneficial for us to know which areas to look.

"In my opinion, since they're a lot of hidden areas in the mansion, try the tunnels. I'm sure he would have them together or in different areas."

“How do you know all of this?” I asked.

Leo smiled. “Milo never knew that my great grandfather built that place. There are still layouts for the ideas that the original owner wanted. Although it was built way before any of our time, I doubt if Milo made any major changes.”

“Wow, this is amazing. Thank you so much,” Zuri said.

“Thank me later. First, we need to get that son of a bitch.”

“I’m with you on that,” I said. I glanced at Zuri who nodded.

Now, we can put our plan into action.

Zuri

After talking for a couple more minutes, the three of us made our way to Milo's compound. I'm not sure why Sergeant Jones didn't mention that he knew someone here, but it was probably a reason for it.

Leo parked down the road from the mansion so we wouldn't be too obvious as Damon glanced at me.

"So, you know what to do?"

I nodded. "Yeah. I'll check the hidden areas in and around the house, including the tunnels."

"You think you'll be able to get in?"

"I'll have to find a way."

"Majority of the tunnels will be hidden. One is in the study, and another one is by his bedroom. Getting in those will be easy, actually getting inside of the house will be the challenge," Leo said.

"Leave that to me," Damon said.

"You still have a bullet wound to think about," I reminded him.

"And I'll be fine."

I sighed, realizing there was no point talking to him about that. He's going to do what he wanted anyway.

We got out of the SUV and followed Leo to the gates. We walked near the back to see if any guards were around. Luckily, there wasn't.

"We have to jump the fence," Damon said.

“I can’t climb this! This is a high-rise fence,” I whispered.

“This is the only way you’re getting in.”

He put his hands out for me to jump up. I held onto the fence as I used my strength to get up to the top. I’m glad this wasn’t one of those fences that’ll electrocute you. I would have been screwed if it was.

I had to jump, and I fell on the ground, scraping my elbow. I got up, brushing myself off as I waited on Leo to come down. Once he did, Damon followed. I could tell he was struggling somewhat as he climbed the wired fence. Although I knew what the problem was, we had to get a move on since we weren’t sure if security was around.

Damon jumped, landing on his feet, which was too sexy. I cleared that thought from my head as I went to the back.

“You have a bobby pin?” he whispered.

“Does it look like I do?”

“Let me,” Leo said and pulled out a pocket knife. He slid it to a long wire to pick the lock.

“How do you know this place doesn’t have an alarm?” I whispered.

“Knowing Milo, it does, but it’s probably not set.”

Or this could be a trap,” I replied.

After minutes of fidgeting with the lock, Leo finally got it open. We slowly walked in, each of us aiming our guns while seeing if anyone was present. Damon looked at the two of us with a determined look.

“We have to split up. I’ll go look for Milo, and you two can find everyone,” Damon said.

"We have to keep a lookout for anyone else that may be here," Leo added. "I do have back up in case we hit a snag."

"Okay, thanks. You sure you'll be okay?" Damon asked me.

I nodded as he looked into my eyes. "Love you, okay?"

"Love you too."

While Damon walked the opposite direction, Leo told me to head upstairs while he went further down the hall. I quickly went up, hoping no one sees me as I walked down the hall, looking for a room that could potentially have a hidden door. I checked into one, which looked like the study, and walked in.

I looked around when I noticed a wall that looked out of place. I went to it, feeling on it to see if there was an opening. Sure enough, I pushed on it and it slowly turned. I looked behind me, making sure no one else was in the room and stepped in. I went down a couple of steps to a secret room. The lights were dimmed as I pushed away a spider web that was in my way. I walked even further when I gasped at the sight before me.

"Oh my God!" I whispered as I saw Nicole bound and strapped up in restraints. Cole was on the floor, which was dirty and full of trash, and he was wailing. I quickly went to him as Nicole was crying. I tried to calm Cole down as I held him, hoping he could so I could find a way to unstrap his mom. He looked into my eyes, having a sense of hope as he touched my face. I nodded, letting him know that everything would be okay as I looked around to see what I could use for Nicole. After two minutes of searching, I found a saw. I looked around for somewhere that Cole could go. I didn't want to put him back on the floor, but I didn't have a choice.

When I did, he started wailing again as I quickly began to free Nicole. I pulled the tape off of her mouth and she let out a small scream. The saw was sharp enough to cut through the restraints, but it was taking a while to do it.

"How did you find us?" Nicole asked.

“It took a while, but had some help from the Belizean officer, Leo.”

“I’m glad someone is going to take that bastard down.”

“Where are my parents and Mr. and Mrs. Scott?”

“They’re in separate rooms. I have no idea where they took them though.”

“We’re going to have to search for them because I’m not leaving here without them.”

“You want to bet on that?”

I looked up and was shocked to see who was standing on the stairs.

Damon

While Zuri and Leo were looking for everyone, my main mission was to find Milo. I wanted to end this once and for all with him, so hopefully, this will end soon.

I looked through various rooms looking for him when I was about to approach a room similar to a library. As soon as I was about to set foot in the room, I felt a gun pressed against my back.

“Stop right there.”

I took a deep breath as I stood there. By the voice, I already knew it was Patrick. If I turned around, I’ll probably get shot, but that’s a chance that I’m willing to make.

I slowly reached to my pocket, when he bent my arm back.

“I suggest you get your hand off me.”

“Ahh, Damon Baxter. How in the hell did you find this place?”

“If you let me go, I can go on my way. In fact, pretend I’m not even here.”

“Why would I even do that? Fucking cop.”

“I guess Malcolm told Milo. How’s life treating him in prison? Has he found a girlfriend yet?”

“I knew you were no good from the start, but Milo wouldn’t listen. Now he has to watch his back even more because of your bitch ass!”

“He brought this on himself. Now, let go of me.”

“And if I don’t?”

I guess he'll have to learn the hard way as I kicked him from behind. I turned around trying to strike him as he blocked my hits. He tried to punch me when I kicked him again, causing him to fall on the floor. He quickly got up and we started to throw out jabs, which ended with him grabbing me and putting me in a chokehold. I was struggling to breathe while he pressed his arms further on my neck. I went into my pocket and found my knife. I stuck it in his thigh, making him release me, and he fell back on the floor.

I stood before him and gave him a heated stare. "I told you to let go of me."

"Fucking prick!"

I used my foot to jam the knife into his thigh, causing him to scream.

"Now, I'm going to walk away. You can't stop me since you have a knife in your thigh. If you attempt to, I will turn around and shoot you in the head. Do you really want that, Patrick?"

"Get this shit out of me!"

I jammed my foot onto the knife again and smiled. "I hope you get some help for that," I suggested and went to the library. He should have known not to mess with me.

I walked with my gun, looking for a light switch. I found it near the side wall and switched it on, revealing Milo sitting behind his desk with a glass of brandy in his hand. I aimed my gun at him, glad that I finally found him.

"Hello son. Glad you could make it."

"I'm not your son. I would never be related to you."

"Oh, but you are. The cats out of the bag now, so there's no point in hiding it."

I glanced at him, noticing we did have a bit of a resemblance, from the black hair to the blue eyes. I always saw it, but I never wanted to admit it.

"You know I can shoot you right here."

"I can do the same," he said as three of his henchmen came out of the corners, aiming their guns at me. I shook my head.

"You know I'll still shoot you."

"I know you will, but as soon as you do, one of these men will do the same to you."

"Can't do your own shit for once. I forgot, you don't want to get your hands dirty, right?"

"You know I'm capable, but why should I when I have people who would do it for me."

I moved closer as the men did the same. I aimed it at one of them.

"I will seriously shoot you, so stand the fuck back."

"Look at you. You really are like me."

"The hell if I am. I'm Austin and Teresa Baxter's son. I could never be like you. You're nothing but a bully who would do anything to get ahead."

"Just like you. You followed in your uncle's footsteps, yet you're doing the same thing as your parents. Cop and a hitman. You should be proud."

"Shut up or this next bullet will go to your chest."

"Go ahead. No one stopping you, but yourself. All of that talking you're doing you could have shot me by now."

"Keep encouraging me and I will."

"But you won't. You know why, because you need me to tell you where your precious Zuri's parents are hiding. By the way, where is your lovely girlfriend?"

"Leave her out of this."

"She was in this regardless, so there's no point in protecting her. Hopefully she's doing well down in the tunnel. It can be very scary down there."

I glared at him as he took out his phone and showed it to me. "I guess that degree you received didn't help you with your street smarts. If you would have known me by now, you would know nothing gets past me."

I sighed. He had a video of Zuri and Nicole in a tunnel with Erin pointing a gun at them.

"I see Erin finally made it out of that room," I said.

"You think you two are slick, coming into my house thinking you could be heroes and rescue everyone. Nothing around here is easy, so you're going to have to earn it."

"We know it won't be easy, but we will walk out of here with everyone that you kidnapped. And you and your lackeys will be in handcuffs. You can join your no good ass brother in prison."

"You're going to have to get through them and me before that will happen. Regardless of how you feel about me, I'm still your blood. You won't do anything to me."

"I just put my uncle in jail, so it's possible."

"He's not your blood. I am. So, we'll see what you'll do to me," he said while coming over to me. I still had my gun on him as he stared at me.

"You are your mother's son. Eager to do whatever is needed to get the job done. You know, your mother was a good woman. Smart, vibrant, and very beautiful. She had this aura about her that made every man want her. Of course, I had my turn with her, which produced you. I thought you would turn out to take over the business. Never did I imagine that you would turn against me."

"Why would you think I wouldn't? I don't want to be anything like you. Just because my mom made a mistake by being with you, doesn't mean you get a pass with me."

"I think you would if you want your girlfriend to stay alive. Or I'll just make it easy for me and get rid of you both. You failed my expectations anyway by not getting rid of Tyrik, so I no longer have any use for you."

"What does it matter anyway? His own father shot him."

"Because he was a traitor, just like you are. Now, if you want to get to her, you have to get through my men, and possibly me. Let's see what you're made of."

I stepped up to him and looked into his eyes. "You don't want to see what I'm capable of."

"I want to. If you love her like you say you do, then you will."

I scoffed, knowing he was being serious. If he wanted a fight, then he got it. It was time to finally settle this once and for all.

Zuri

"I see you finally made it out of that room," I said while looking at Erin.

"You wish I was still in there, little bitch."

"Listen, I'm not trying to cause any problems. I'm just going to take Nicole and Cole and we'll be on our way," I said as I picked up Cole.

"Move one more step and I will shoot you and that brat," she said while aiming the gun at me.

"And I'll kill you with my bare hands," Nicole said as she tried to get to her, but I held her back.

"No, Nicole, let me," I said.

Even though she still had the gun on me, I stepped up to her, ready to go. If she wanted to do something, then I was ready.

"You know, I have had about enough of you. Not only have you hurt me in the worst possible way, but you're standing here acting as if you're the damn victim. So if I have to beat your muthafucking ass right here, then I will do so."

"What are you waiting for then?" Erin said. She still had the gun, which I pushed away from her and it fell on the ground.

"If you're a real bitch, then you wouldn't need the gun. Come and fight me."

"Fine, let's go."

She put her hands up in fists as I took a swing at her. She ducked as I took another swing, landing on her jaw. She tried to hit me, but I put her down on the floor and started hitting her. She blocked my punches as she pulled her hands up. She pushed herself up and kicked me across my chin, which caused me to fall on the ground. She got on top of me and tried to hit me, but I grabbed her hands and pinned them above my head.

"Knowing your ass, you probably like this."

"You wish," Erin said.

I pushed her on the ground, tired of playing with her and began my attack. My mind flash backed to that night and what she had done. I continued swinging on her as she took every blow I was throwing. Her ass deserved so much more than what I was doing, but if this is what it took to get her off our back, then so be it.

I continued beating her ass when I noticed she was growing unconscious. I was still going when Nicole told me to stop. I knew I should, but I was still upset over everything that she had done. She was supposed to have been my friend, but she double crossed me in the worst way.

I put in one more punch before getting up and kicking her in the side. She was completely knocked out, which meant we had time to get out.

"You think she'll wake up?" Nicole asked.

I shrugged. "I could care less if she does. Let's get out of here."

I helped Nicole and Cole up the steps and to the hallway. Just as soon as I was approaching the corner, I saw Leo and an officer come to us.

"I'm glad you're okay. Milo has cameras all around, so he knows what happened."

"Typical of him."

"I was able to find your parents-in-law, Nicole. One of the officers was able to get them out safely."

"Wow, thank you. And Milo didn't do anything?"

"Surprisingly, no. I think he has a bigger agenda in mind for Zuri and Damon. He just used everyone as bait to lure you two here."

"I wouldn't be surprised if he did."

"I'll get you and your son out of here, okay?"

"Thank you. What about you, Zuri?"

"Don't worry about me. I have to find Damon. Just take Cole and get out of here."

"Just be safe, okay? Damon as well. I can't lose you two."

"And you won't, sweetie. We'll see you out there."

She nodded and I went the opposite direction down the hall. I followed the monitors as I looked for the room that Damon and Milo were in. He was fighting one of Milo's men, which had my blood pumping. We have to get through this so we can find my parents. They have to be here, so why haven't they been found?

I was finally able to find the room as I burst through the door. One of the guys was guarding of the door as he tried to hit me. I grabbed a letter opener nearby and tried to stab him, but he grabbed me, pulling me towards him. I looked at Damon as he stared at me in disbelief. He didn't have to worry, because now, I was ready to help him.

I still had the opener in my hand as I slashed his upper thigh. He let go of me as I turned around and slashed his throat. Blood was spilling onto my shirt as I watched him fall to the floor. That only made Milo even more pissed as he urged another one of his men to come towards me.

"Here!" Damon yelled as he kicked his gun over to me. He was handling his own with two of the guys as the other tried to come to me. I quickly picked up the gun and began shooting at him. One bullet hit his chest, while the other went to his leg. He fell down as I tried to help Damon, but Milo grabbed me. I shrugged to get out of his hold when Damon tried to come to me. That's when Milo pulled out a knife and held it to my throat.

"Make one more step and I will cut her throat open."

Damon stepped back and Milo smiled.

"I got you where I want you now."

I pulled my arm back and punched him in his gut. He hovered over, causing the knife to fall on the floor, and I kicked it over to Damon. He grabbed his gun and aimed it at Milo.

"We can keep playing this game all day, but you're going to tell us where you have Zuri's parents."

"Like hell I will," he choked out.

I began hitting him as Damon pulled me away from him. He stared at him as Milo smiled.

"You are an ungrateful son of a bitch. You betrayed me, the organization, and most of all, your parents."

Damon looked at me and I nodded. There was another way for us to know where my parents were being kept. I just have to get over to Milo's desk to switch the cameras.

While Damon was distracting Milo, I walked backwards over to the desk. I looked at the computer and saw the different angles around the house. I didn't know for sure which room was what, but I had to quickly find out. I glanced towards camera #14 and saw my dad slumped over, while my mom was looking up. She must have known a camera was in the room. From the looks of it, they were in another tunnel.

I looked over and saw Milo staring directly at me. Damon pushed him as I ran out of the room.

"You little bitch!" Milo yelled as I headed down the hall. I heard gunshots as I looked behind me, hoping those sounds didn't come from the library. Instead, it came from two men who were chasing me. I knew I should have grabbed something on the way out. There was plenty ammo around the floor.

I turned the corner, praying that I was going in the right direction, and looked behind me. They were still following me. I have to find a way to get rid of them.

I heard another gunshot, but this time, one of the men fell down. I saw Damon coming towards the other, shooting him in the groin. He immediately fell down as Damon came to me.

"Here, you're going to need this," he said, while giving me a pistol.

"What happened to Milo?"

"Don't worry about him, but we do need to find your parents and get the hell out of here."

I nodded and we ran down the hall. From what Leo mentioned, there had to be another room with a hidden door to another tunnel. I thought it was in the library, but I didn't notice when we were there.

"I saw them in another tunnel, but we have to figure out where the tunnel is."

"You found the one in the study, right?"

"Yeah, and there wasn't a hidden door in the library?"

"No."

We continued going down the hallway until I stopped at a room on the far end. For some reason, it stood out from the rest as I looked at the door. I slowly opened it and walked inside. Damon was behind me as he tried to find a light switch, but couldn't. I found my phone and turned on the flashlight. At least this one that Leo gave me had apps that worked.

We looked ahead and saw there were a couple of stairs going up. We took them two at a time, which directed us to another door. We opened it and walked inside to find my parents tied up to a pole in the back of the room.

"Oh my God! Zuri!" my mom yelled as I ran over to her.

I looked at the rope, trying to find something to break them with. Damon looked around and sighed.

"He would do this."

"What the hell is going on? One minute we were having fun at the resort, and the next, someone grabbed us and knocked us out," my dad said. Even though he sounded weak throughout that entire statement, he was still trying to be tough.

"That's nothing you need to worry about right now. We just need to get out of here," Damon said as he noticed something shiny in the corner. He ran to it as I looked at my parents. They looked to be malnourished, so there's no telling how long they were down here. I wanted to cry, but I had to be strong. If Damon didn't kill Milo, I will definitely do so in a heartbeat. He has played with too many people's lives and it was time he was stopped.

Damon came over with a sharp piece of glass and started to work on getting the rope off of my dad first. As soon as we're able to get out of here, they needed to go to the hospital. My dad looked as if he needed the most medical attention.

"Hopefully this will work," he said as he continued. I put my hands together in prayer mode, asking God to help us get through this. I knew one thing for sure, we had to move quickly before someone saw us on the camera and found us.

"Damon, we need to hurry."

"I'm trying."

I kept a lookout at the door as he continued. A few minutes later, and he was able to take it off of my dad. He gave the glass to me as I started on my mom. As I cut through, a piece slit on my hand, causing me to flinch, but I kept going. I had to finish.

Damon held on to my dad as he gave him a perplexed look.

"What type of trouble you got my daughter into? First, she showed up to our house with you, then had us travel all around the damn world, you all disappeared, and then we're here in a damn dungeon with you two having guns. You got her caught up in a drug ring, do you?"

"Dad, you're sick, and that's what you're worried about? You should be grateful we found you."

"Which we are, baby," my mom said.

I was finally able to get her out as I grabbed a hold of her. We all went up the stairs to the first room, hoping that no one was waiting on us. Surprisingly, no one was. Damon looked down the hall before signaling me to follow.

"We have to find Leo so he can get your parents. We still have unfinished business with Milo."

"What do you mean unfinished business?"

"I just knocked him out long enough for us to find your parents. I'm sure he's up and looking for us now. We have to get them out before he finds us."

We went towards the hall and to the door, when the alarm went off.

"How convenient," Damon said.

We went through the doors and saw Leo running to us.

"I tried to go back in, but I couldn't. I think he locked the doors from the inside."

"He pulled the alarms to know when we were leaving," Damon said while handing my dad to Leo.

"What are you doing?" my dad yelled.

"This is an officer with Belize police. He'll take care of you and your wife."

"Where are we going?" my mom asked.

"You'll both be going to the hospital. Damon and I will be okay."

"Zuri—"

"Mom, please. Just go."

"Zuri Caldwell, you better come with us," my dad said before falling over.

"Dad, please go. I have to do this."

"You don't have to do anything. He put you in this mess, so let him deal with it."

"Sir, we have to go," Leo advised.

My dad looked at me as I followed Damon to the opposite direction of the mansion. He looked at me and I sighed.

"We'll talk about that later."

We went over to the garden and saw two guys coming over to us. I looked behind us and saw three more. This was getting ridiculous.

"Where's Milo?" Damon asked.

That was the big question as he was nowhere to be found, but his goons were visibly present as he took my hand and led me towards a wooded area. We ran down the dirt path, trying to get as far away from them as we could. We heard gunshots as we continued running. Since we were outnumbered, there was no point in shooting back, but if we have to, we will.

"Should we hide somewhere?"

"Where?" Damon asked while looking ahead.

We were getting close to the end as we ended near a cliff that connected to a river. I looked down, wondering what the hell we were about to do.

"You can't be serious."

"Does it look like I'm kidding?"

"I'm not jumping."

"As you can see, there are no other options, Zuri. We have to jump."

I looked down again as my anxiety started to go into overdrive. This was some bullshit.

Are you ready?"

I glanced at Damon, feeling completely terrified of what we were about to do. He held my hand, squeezing it while his blue eyes stared into mine. I looked behind me, wondering if we were still being chased, but luckily, Damon found a way to get them off our trail.

He flashed that smile of his that made my pussy wet. This is not the time to be thinking about that, especially when they're people trying to kill us.

"You know I got you, right?"

I nervously nodded. “I know. I trust you.”

We heard gunshots as I looked behind me. Damon pulled me to the edge, yelling we have to go. I gave a silent prayer, asking God to keep us safe as I closed my eyes, not wanting to look where I was heading.

“Zuri, let’s go!”

I quickly opened them as we jumped off the edge of the cliff, heading towards the rushing waters, hoping we don’t die.

As my body hit the water, I couldn’t help but to feel a bit excited. That was definitely a rush. I probably wouldn’t do it again, but at least I knew I could handle it.

I looked over to see if Damon was near me, but he wasn’t. I pushed myself up to see if he could be on land, but he was nowhere to be found.

“Damon!” I yelled as I looked around before going back under. I swam, trying to find him, but no such luck.

I came back up, giving myself a bit of air as I screamed his name. He can’t do this. We came too far for him to do this.

“Baby, please, if you can, answer me!”

I started to panic as I went down again to find him. Could his wound had bothered him to swim? He has been pushing himself when he knew he shouldn’t have. I continued to look for him when I found him floating underneath a couple of rocks. My heart started pounding as I went to him. I tried to push him out, but he was too heavy. I found my inner strength as I slowly dragged him over to dry land and tilted his head back. I checked his pulse and it was a little faint.

I stared to perform CPR, hoping he’d wake up. But if he does, we are in the middle of nowhere, so it would be hard for Leo or anyone to locate us.

“Come on baby, wake up for me, please.”

I continued, praying that he’ll open those pretty eyes of his. That’s one of the things I love about him. Hell, I love everything about him and I would probably lose my mind if he doesn’t regain consciousness.

I was giving him mouth to mouth when I felt his tongue going into my mouth. My eyes widened as he pulled on my lips, having all sorts of emotions go through me. I pulled away and he weakly laughed.

“That’s a good way to wake me up.”

“You jerk!”

He laughed again and I hugged him. “For a minute there, I thought I lost you.”

“You will never lose me, Z. I’m not going anywhere.”

I smiled and he slowly kissed me. We stared at each other when we heard a helicopter. I quickly jumped up, hoping to flag whoever down. I waved my hands in the air as a rope was coming down. I tried to see if I could get a look at the pilot, but couldn’t. I wondered if this was a good idea since we didn’t know who the hell was rescuing us. However, if we don’t go, we might not be found again.

I took the initiative and went closer as the rope lowered. The person stuck his head out and I gave a sigh of relief.

"Are you both okay?” Leo yelled.

“Damon might need to go to the hospital.”

“I’ll see if we can make landing. Hold on!”

I nodded as the pilot maneuvered the helicopter as it attempted to make a safe landing. I went over to Damon and smiled.

"At least we were quickly found."

"Yeah. I don't need to go to the hospital."

"You know you do."

"We need to find Milo."

"We will, but you need to get better."

Leo came out of the helicopter and helped me get Damon inside. I got in as well, as I held his hand. I stared into his eyes and touched his hair.

"Don't worry, we'll get Milo. He's not going to walk away from this."

Damon nodded and I put his head against my chest. After everything that bastard has done, I'll make sure he doesn't get away with this. Even if I have to take him out myself.

Damon

Once we were airlifted, we were taken to Belize Medical Associates where I was kept overnight for observation. The doctor also had to check on my wound, which surprisingly was healing just fine.

The doctor did suggest that I get some rest, which I will, once I find Milo. I also found out that Zuri was checked in, but was released this morning. She said she was fine, but from the tone of her voice, something was up. I guess I would have to find out what's going on later.

Zuri's parents were also in the hospital as they both were treated for exhaustion and dehydration. I found out from Zuri that Milo had kept them there for almost two weeks with barely any food or water. Nicole, Cole, and Chandler's parents were also in the hospital being treated for the same aliments. I knew that was hard for them and once I can get out of this bed, I'll go back on my hunt of finding him.

I'm sure he fled Belize by now, which Leo mentioned he was going to work around the clock to search for him and have him captured. He also placed officers around my room as well as Zuri's parents, Nicole, and Chandler's parents in case anything happens.

There was a knock at the door and Zuri walked in. She gave a beautiful smile, which made me do the same. She held onto the door as she wheeled her father in, which had me surprised. He gave me a stern look as Zuri's expression changed from happy to apologetic.

"Even though he should be in bed, he wanted to come see you."

"How did he get through security?"

"Don't even ask."

"I'm not letting no doctor from another country look at me," he said and coughed.

I shook my head. This man is ridiculous.

“Well, you have no choice at the moment. Why can’t you be like Mom and be cooperative?”

"Your mom doesn’t give a shit about anything. She can have a hack work on her, but I prefer someone in my home country.”

“Hello, Mr. Caldwell. I’m glad you’re doing better.”

He rolled his eyes at me and Zuri sighed.

“I came here to talk to you. What in the hell did you get my daughter into? And you better tell me.”

I slowly sat up in the bed and stared at her father. I might not like him, but I have to respect him.

“There’s a lot that has to be explained.”

“Hell, I have time, so go ahead and talk.”

“Okay, but first, I need to get this off my chest. Despite how you feel about me, I love your daughter and will do everything in my power to make her happy.”

He still gave me the death stare as I told the entire story, even going back to when we first met five years ago, minus the one-night stand and me being a T.A. He didn’t need to know that.

While I talked, he was still giving me that stare, but I wasn’t backing down. No matter who was in my way, I will fight for Zuri, so I will make it known that I’m not going anywhere.

“You put my daughter through a lot of shit.”

“Dad, it wasn’t just him. I would have been in the crossfire regardless since I witnessed a murder. That’s how everything was set into motion on my end.”

"Yeah, by him."

"You can't blame it all on Damon. Tyrik's dad is a notorious crime boss who steals and kills for a living. Despite knowing the entire truth, you are still being negative towards Damon. He's a cop who is trying to do his job and you could care less."

"It's not that, Zuri. He lied to you."

"Everyone tells a lie every now and then. I lied to Damon too, so I'm not exactly innocent. All I asked of you is to stop holding this grudge towards him. He hasn't done anything wrong."

"Mr. Caldwell, as I mentioned, I love Zuri and I'm letting you know that I'm not going anywhere, so you're going to have to get used to seeing me."

"You're not going anywhere? Do you hear him talking to me like this, Zuri?"

"I'm not being disrespectful, I'm just stating a fact."

"If I wasn't in this damn chair I'll knock your ass out."

"Dad, stop it! He's not going anywhere, especially since I'm carrying his child!"

I stared at her while her dad gave a disappointed look. He shook his head and sighed.

"You're pregnant? How far along are you?" I asked.

"Just two weeks. I noticed I haven't been feeling well, but I just thought it was because of everything that was happening."

"The doctor just confirmed it?"

"Yes, baby. They drew blood and it came up. Believe me, I'm just as shocked as you are. Now you'll get to experience being a father."

I leaned back, still surprised, when I looked at Mr. Caldwell.

"Take me back to my room, Zuri."

"Dad…"

"Take me back. I can't and I *won't* celebrate this."

Zuri looked as if she was about to cry, which pissed me off. I couldn't take anymore of her dad's behavior.

"You know what Mr. Caldwell, you're truly being a bigot right now."

"Excuse me! Don't you talk to me like that!"

"But you are. Ever since Zuri introduced me to you, you have given every snide remark and dirty look every chance you got and it's pissing me off. Have you even noticed how upset she is right now? Of course you don't because you're thinking about your own damn feelings and what people will say about her having a biracial child."

"You have a lot of nerve talking to me like this."

"Someone should. I held back on saying anything, but I can't anymore. You're hurting your daughter and I'm not going to continue to watch you do that to her. When she's hurting, I'm hurting too, and that's something I never want her to do.

"I know I have put her in harm's way, and I know how concerned you are. I am too, but I had a job to do, and even though it's still not done, I will do everything possible to protect her. She is my life, Mr. Caldwell, and I want you and whoever else to know that we will continue building a life together, whether you like it or not."

He gave me that death stare again and looked away.

"Take me to my room please, Zuri."

She slowly nodded and turned him to face the door. She looked back at me and gave a sad look before wheeling him out.

I took a deep breath, wishing it didn't have to go that far, but I couldn't sit back and continue listening to him. I just hope I haven't ruined my relationship with Zuri.

Zuri

I wheeled my dad back to his room while trying to hold back my tears. What Damon said was what I've been telling my dad for years. He's a good man, but he has a lot of views that he needed to change, especially now since he's about to be a grandfather. Even when I was pregnant the first time, that was one of the issues that bothered me. Although I love my dad, unless he changes his ways, I can't allow him to be around my son or daughter.

Instead of taking him to his room, I took him to my mom's room. In Damon's room, I wasn't going to say that I was pregnant, it sort of slipped out. I already knew that since my dad knows, then I had to tell my mom too.

I opened the door to see her sitting up in the bed. She was drinking a cup of water as she slowly turned her head to us.

"What are you doing out of bed?"

"You know he doesn't listen to anyone, Mom."

"I told you to take me back to my room," he said angrily.

"What's he upset about now? I swear, your ass always mad. You probably came into the world with a scowl on your face."

"Why did you marry me then if I'm always so bitter?"

"Because I love your angry ass."

"Your daughter has something to say," he said while looking at me.

"I'm pregnant, Mom."

She looked at me with tears in her eyes. "Oh baby. I'm so happy for you. Damon is the father, isn't he?"

"Of course, Mom."

"Humph," my dad scoffed.

"And of course you have a problem with it?" she asked my dad.

"Damn right. That means she will never get rid of him. He'll be in our lives forever."

"Clyde, stop."

"He put this entire family in danger. What makes you think he'll even be a good father? That child will be ridiculed every day of his life because of the decisions his parents made."

"Yes, him or her will be ridiculed because of people like you who don't want to accept change."

My dad shook his head. "So you're going to tell me off too?"

"I don't have to say much since Damon said it all. I do have a promise and that is if you can't change your ways, you will never see your grandchild."

He looked at me speechless while my mom gave a sad look.

"Zuri."

"I'm serious, Dad. If you can't accept my relationship with Damon, then you won't accept our child."

"That's not true."

"Yes, it is. How you're talking now, you'll instill those views towards our child and that's teaching hate. Our child will already be facing ignorance from other people, he or she doesn't need that from their own flesh and blood. Instead, they need love and encouragement. That's all I want and the way your behavior is, you're not going to supply that."

"Zuri, I just want what's best for you. I don't think he's that."

"Damon is who I want. Yes, we had our shares of ups and downs, but it was because of me being one-sided. I know that we will face even more battles ahead, but that's okay because we will always have each other's backs. That's something I hope you'll understand one day."

I went to the call button to page a nurse to come in. They didn't even know he was out of his room since I snuck him out. One of the orderlies left the wheelchair in his room, that's how he was able to get out.

The door opened and a nurse quickly walked in, talking in Kriol, so I already knew she was upset with my dad.

As we watched him being wheeled off, my mom looked at me and smiled. "Despite your dad being pissed, I am happy that you're pregnant. That will surely be a beautiful baby."

I smiled. "Thank you. I just want to make things right, not just for Damon and me, but even for Dad. I know he probably thinks I'm a disappointment."

"Why would you think that? Your father loves you."

"I have made a lot of bad decisions in my life. From being involved with Tyrik and making an ass out of myself during an event, to even lying to Damon."

"About what?"

I took a deep breath, wondering if I should even go there about the abortion, but I needed to talk to someone about it besides Nicole. If I confessed to my mom, I knew she wouldn't judge me.

"Damon and I met five years ago and we had a one-night stand. I didn't think I was going to see him again until he was in my economics class as the professor."

"Wow, he's a professor. Sexy and smart."

I smiled and continued. "We had a relationship for a few months, until I winded up pregnant and got the job at Randall. I didn't tell him. Instead, I went to L.A. and got an abortion. I finally did fess up about the baby, only to tell him that I miscarried. Erin opened her big mouth and told Damon the truth."

My mom leaned back in the bed and shook her head. "Aww baby, why would you do that to him?"

"Because I was scared. I didn't want people to judge me because I had a child from someone that I didn't even know at the time."

"Were you more worried about him being white and what people would have thought about your relationship?"

I shook my head. "No. I didn't care if people had a problem with that. It was more of me not being able to handle the fact that I was going to be a mother."

"How do you feel about it now?"

"I'm ready for it. It'll definitely be an adjustment, but it'll be a great experience."

"Zuri, we all make mistakes in our lives, that's what makes us human. What we do know is that we're able to learn from them so we won't make those mistakes again. I think for you, you're doing that right now."

"When Damon found out the actual truth, the hurt he had in his eyes was something I never want to see again. I don't want to hurt him like that again."

"And you won't. You love that man too much to. I still can't believe all of this stemmed from one night together."

"Relationships have to start from somewhere."

"That's true. I'm just happy that you two have worked things out and are moving forward with your life together."

"Me too."

"As for your dad, he will come around, sweetie. Once he sees his grandchild, he will forget about everything and love him or her unconditionally.

"I really hope so," I gave a tiny smile, but in the back of my mind, I didn't believe that for a second.

***

Once I talked to my mom for a few minutes, I went back to Damon's room where he was watching TV. He looked over and smiled. "Hey baby."

"Hey. I'm really sorry about earlier."

"Why are you apologizing? It's your dad who is being difficult."

"But I didn't want to tell you like that."

"You did and I'm still happy about it. I just wish Milo was caught so we can all be safe."

"Which we will. Everything will work out and we'll be happy and raise our boy or girl. There is one thing though."

"What's that?"

“I can’t help but to think about the child that I aborted. I still feel guilty about that and I’m sorry.”

“Zuri, that’s something that we will get through together. That will still take some time to heal, but I’m not going to punish you for it.”

“You should.”

“What’s done is done now. We can’t go back in time. If we could, then there would be a lot of things that we would fix or erase.”

“That’s true. I told my mom everything. From how we met, to the abortion.”

He gave an understanding look. “I’m sure she said not to beat yourself up about everything.”

“She did. She gave some sound advice about the entire situation. And of course she’s happy that we’re doing better with everything.”

“I’m assuming she wasn’t a Tyrik fan?”

“She liked him, but she knew that he wasn’t the one for me.”

“Mothers have that intuition about everything. But just know that I love you regardless and that I always will.”

“I love you too.”

I bent down and kissed him. He looked into my eyes and smiled.

“You will make a great mom.”

“You think so?”

“I know so. Now me as a father, that’s hard to imagine.”

“I don’t think so. You’ll be fine, D.”

He started to yawn and I kissed him again before going to a chair nearby the window. I grabbed a blanket nearby and wrapped it around me. I looked ahead at him before my eyes drifted off to sleep.

Damon

After Zuri told me to go to sleep, I actually did. That's something I haven't really done lately, so those few hours did me some good. I slowly opened my eyes and saw that the sun was setting and Zuri was gone. I sat up and looked around, wondering if she went to the bathroom. I got out of bed slowly and went to see, but it was dark.

She could have gone to see Nicole or her parents, so I was trying not to worry, but for some reason, from the way her chair was turned and the blanket on the floor, something was up. I looked to see if the officers were still in place through the tiny window when my anxiety kicked into overdrive. Since we were all in danger, Leo pulled some strings and specifically asked for us to be placed in rooms away from other patients. Therefore, no one would know if anything occurred. Case in point, right now.

The two guards that were outside my room were knocked out. It looked as if they were pistol whipped. I looked around and checked to see if either one was still armed. Luckily, one was as I retrieved his gun from his ankle cuff. That's probably why it was still on him. I yanked it, causing me to fall on the floor. I got up and immediately had to hold onto the wall. I was becoming light-headed, which I didn't need right now. Milo has Zuri and I needed to find them, but first, I needed some clothes.

I went to the supply closet and grabbed a pair of scrubs before heading back out. I didn't have a clue on where to go, but I couldn't stand around and wait. I needed to find him before he does try to flee the country.

I went to a phone near the lobby and contacted Leo. Once I was able to, he told me not to go after Milo, but of course, I wasn't going to listen. I hung up and went to the stairs while thinking of areas that Milo could have gone to. I thought about the roof and went up the stairs.

My vision became blurry as I continued. I shook my head to remain focus, which helped a little.

I went up three more flights of stairs, finally getting to the top. I opened the door, seeing a helicopter on the launch pad, and Milo had Zuri at gun point, pulling her hair, threatening her to go on. I went closer to them, aiming my gun at Milo.

"I suggest you stop, muthafucker."

Milo looked at me and smiled. "Glad you were able to make it to the party, Damon. We would have missed you. "

"Let her go!"

"Why should I listen to you? I'm going to use her as leverage to get what I want!"

"You already have what you want. You got your brother and nephew out of the way, so you're on top now!"

"You could take the reins too if you wanted. You could be like your parents and take over the business."

"I don't want the business! Why would I when I don't want anything to do with you. You killed my parents and my best friend. You tortured everyone that I care about, so why would I want any part of what you're dealing?"

He pulled Zuri tighter, which had my fingers itching on the trigger. But there was a slight problem, my vision was blurry and I was seeing two of them.

"If you want her, you're going to have to shoot me!"

I waved my gun, trying to figure out which was the real Milo. Zuri gave a scared look as I noticed he had another gun on the side of his hip. I gave Zuri eye contact, letting her know to grab the gun. Hopefully she'll understand what I meant.

She looked at me and realized what I was doing. She stood still, but her eyes were telling me she got it. I distracted Milo by shooting my gun in the air, causing him to flinch. She quickly grabbed his gun and shot him in the foot. He let Zuri go as he fell down. She aimed it at him as I walked over to the two.

"You dirty bitch."

She fired again, hitting his other foot.

"Call me a bitch again and see where I shoot next."

"I see he has taught you well."

"Maybe so, but I was willing to shoot you."

"That's fine, because you two will never get rid of me. I'll continue to terrorize you, your family, and your kids. I'll make all of your lives a living hell."

"Oh really," I said while looking at Zuri. "You thinking what I'm thinking?"

Zuri nodded. We grabbed Milo and walked him over to the ledge. He glanced at us and laughed.

"You would kill your father?"

I put him on the ledge and looked him in the eyes. "With a father like you, yes I would. I will finally be done with you and everything that you have caused. Maybe now everyone that you terrorized can have a bit of peace and the people you killed can have justice."

"You really are like me if you're ready to kill me."

"I'm nothing like you. I'm doing my civic duty and getting rid of people like you. No one will miss you. In fact, people will probably be cheering for your demise."

"Don't be surprise if people come looking for you, especially Malcolm."

I shrugged. "I doubt it, especially since you have done nothing to help him. Besides, if anyone does, then I'll be ready for them too. Hope you rot in hell, muthafucker."

I pushed him off the ledge as we watched him fall to the bottom, landing on the concrete. Zuri turned her head at the sight of him on the ground, his head spilt open. Several pedestrians witnessed what happened as several screamed or ran. Others just stood near his body.

I held Zuri as she was shaking. I knew these past couple of weeks have taken a toll on her. Hopefully now she can relax a little and start to enjoy her life now.

She pulled away from me and looked out to the sky, closing her eyes and sighing.

"Is it finally over?"

I walked up to her, not sure if it really was. Even though Milo is dead, there's still Malcolm, but I I'm sure he won't be leaving prison anytime soon.

"Yeah, it is."

As we heard the sirens below, we turned towards the door to head back inside. After months of dodging bullets, blows, and crazy people, it was now safe to say that we were finally in the clear. For how long, I don't know, but we're going to enjoy the moment we have together and if anything does happen, like I said to Milo before his demise, I'll be ready for anything and anyone. At least I know I won't be alone. I'll have my girl by my side.

<u>***Zuri***</u>

Two Years Later…

"Baby, did you call the sitter yet? The concert starts in three hours," Damon asked while walking into the living room. I was in the kitchen trying to get Damon Jr., or DJ, his dinner, but instead I was wearing it since he threw it back at me.

"I don't get how he does so well with you during dinner, but with me, he wants to play around."

"Because we have that male bond going. We can relate to each other."

"Oh shut up," I said and playfully shoved him. He put me in his arms and smiled.

"You better be glad DJ is here or you would be bent over on the counter right now."

"Is that all you think about?"

"No. I imagine you on the couch, in the shower, on the stairs."

"Perv."

"You know you want to."

"You know me so well," I said and laughed.

After what happened in Belize, no one suspected that we had anything to do with Milo's death. Everyone just believed that he fell off the ledge, so we kept our mouths shut ever since. We didn't need anyone poking around, so that story will stick with us until the day we die.

With everyone battling their various injuries, we were able to return to the states to try to live our regular lives, but it was hard to, especially since so much had happened. Although Damon returned to his position as a detective, he decided to take a leave of absence to continue teaching. Since we were having a baby, he didn't want to put our lives, or our child's life, in danger. He does get called in to be on special assignments, which I didn't mind, since they were cases that didn't involve crime lords or murder for hire plots.

As for myself, since I couldn't find a job in my field, I decided to open my own event planning company. To do it, I had to get financial backing. I have two partners. Nicole, who was eager to be a business owner, and my dad. With him, that was surprising since he's so stingy with his money, but I think he was still feeling guilty over what happened in Belize that he wanted to make things right. As for him and Damon, things have gotten better between the two. Honestly, they had to since we were now married.

Two weeks after we all returned, Damon asked my dad for my hand in marriage. Although he was still hesitant at the time, he finally started to see that Damon really does love me. He even apologized for his behavior and thanked him for saving his life. Through the power of prayer, I knew things would turn around for him.

During the wedding, my dad was thrilled to walk me down the aisle, which had me in tears. Damon and I said our vows in front of our friends and family at the church that I grew up in. And Damon, wow, that man never looked as good as he did that day. I showed him my appreciation by doing him in the limo. Whenever the mood strikes, I'm always ready, and he found that out plenty of times. Now the three of us were living the suburban life, with the white picket fence and SUV. We're not at the minivan stage yet, but even if we were, that would be a no-go for us.

Damon's phone started to ring as I continued with DJ. I pulled out my phone, wondering if my parents would watch DJ. They were supposed to have a date night at home, but I figured DJ would be asleep, so that shouldn't affect their evening. This night was important for Damon and me because this was the anniversary of the first day we met eight years ago. We always try to celebrate it, whether it's a night out or us watching a movie at home. We never missed the opportunity to celebrate it, especially tonight since we had tickets to see The Weeknd. He's my favorite and when I knew he was coming, I begged Damon for us to go. Of course he agreed. He can't say no to me.

He looked at me and sighed. "Huh baby, I have to leave for a little bit."

"Where are you going? We do have a concert to go to."

"I'll be back. Besides, we still don't have anyone to watch DJ, so we might not even be going."

"Don't talk like that. We're going to see The Weeknd."

"If I didn't know any better, you like him more than me."

I smiled. "You know that's not true."

While DJ was watching TV, Damon pulled me to him and walked me to the corner. One of his hands were going under my shirt, while the other was unbuttoning my shorts.

"What if DJ sees us?"

"He's watching TV. Besides, I couldn't go another second without making you cum."

His finger was slowly rubbing my clit as I buried my face into the crook of his neck. I sucked on his skin, gently biting it, which made him moan in my ear.

"Keep doing that and I'll make you cum another way."

"Is that a promise?"

He grinned as my hands were moving down his back. His finger was a good way to get me off, but it wasn't a substitute for him, which I was craving right now. I couldn't wait until later for us to be alone.

"Come on baby, let me see you cum."

His speed increased as my fingers clawed his back. My legs were growing weak as I bit his neck again, letting him know I was there. He slapped my ass and smiled.

"I can't wait until later."

"Neither can I. And this time, I'll be the one in control."

"That I wouldn't mind at all."

He kissed me before looking at me. "I have to go, but I promise you, I'll be back in time."

I nodded. "Okay. I'll call my mom to see if she can watch DJ."

"Cool. Let me know."

He pulled me to him, giving me a passionate kiss before slowly letting my hand go. I stared at him, wondering if something was wrong.

"Is everything okay?"

He nodded. "Yeah, everything is cool."

I watched him leave, wondering where he was going. For some reason, it felt as if he was walking away and never coming back.

***

Once I called my mom and asked if she could watch DJ, her and my dad came, which I was grateful for. The two told me to get ready, so I did. I wanted to get my eyebrows done, so I went to the spa nearby the house for a quick thread. After I was done, I was going to the parking lot when I heard someone call my name. I looked around until I saw Tyrik standing on the other side of the lot. I went over to him and he gave me a huge smile. I didn't notice him holding on to a little girl who looked to be about three years old.

"Hey. Wow, I was just thinking about you the other day. How are you?" I asked while giving him a hug.

"Everything is good. I quit Randall and went into my own business, but as a PR firm."

"Oh really. You know Nicole will have a fit with that."

He laughed. "Nicole will be alright. Besides, there's nothing wrong with a little friendly competition."

I smiled. "Definitely not."

"Tell Nicole despite our differences, I apologize for what my family has put her through. No one deserved what they did to any of us."

I nodded. "I agree."

"But how is she?"

"She's good. Besides her job, she's dating again. In fact, she's back with her ex, Malik."

"Didn't he always used to cheat on her?"

I nodded. "Yeah, but he's a changed man now, which I have to admit he has."

"That's good. I'm happy for her. And congrats on your wedding. I knew you were saving your marriage card for Damon."

"Maybe I was, but it doesn't take away what we had. I really did care about you. Even when everyone doubted you about being involved with Milo and Malcolm, deep down I knew you weren't."

"Thank you for keeping your faith in me."

"Of course. And who is this sweetheart right here?" I asked while giving a bright smile.

"Let me introduce you to my daughter, Iesha. Iesha, this is my good friend, Zuri."

She waved and I smiled. "She is too cute. And that hair! Who knew you could produce a gorgeous child?"

"Real funny, Z. But she's my pride and joy. I love her to death."

"Is Christette her mom, or…"

"Hey," Christette said as she came over and gave Tyrik a kiss. She looked at me and smiled. "Hey Zuri, it's nice to see you."

"Likewise, Christette."

She looked at the two of us and took Iesha's hand. "Sweetie, why don't we give Daddy and Zuri some time alone, okay?"

She nodded and the two left. I looked at Tyrik, wondering what was going on.

"Okay, what's going on? Christette left in a hurry."

Tyrik looked around and sighed. "There was one thing I didn't tell you."

"And what was that?"

He cleared his throat and gave me an apologetic look. "Erin is Iesha's mom."

I gave him a crazed look, wondering if he was joking. "What?"

"I'm sorry, Zuri, but I was seeing her while I was with you. Believe me, I didn't know what she was doing with my dad or Milo. I think she was with me to distract me so I wouldn't have known."

"Let me get this straight. You cheated on me with that nasty stank and got her pregnant? Wow."

"Zuri, I'm sorry, but we were growing apart and I knew you still had feelings for Damon. That's why I did what I did."

"I should have known. I mean, the signs were there. So you were talking about yourself that night at the restaurant?"

"Maybe I was."

"I should be mad at you, but I'm not. I'm perfectly happy now, so your past mistakes are not a factor to me. Now if we were still together and you pulled this shit, then yes, I would have literally killed you."

"And I believe it."

"Where is that stank anyway?"

"She passed away last year. She was shot in her apartment during an argument."

I shook my head. I should feel bad about that, but I honestly wasn't. Sometimes karma can bite you in the ass and with her, it was ten times over.

"When Erin died, Christette took over and officially became Iesha's mom. She signed the papers the other day."

I nodded. "I commend her for that."

"She loves Iesha. And if you're wondering, we're engaged."

"Congrats. So Erin was pregnant during everything?"

Tyrik nodded. "Yeah, she was."

I sighed, realizing I could have killed their child. Tyrik realized what I was thinking and sighed.

"Don't beat yourself over that. Iesha is here, so everything is fine."

"What about Malcolm? I know he received life in prison, but have you talked to him?"

Tyrik shook his head. "No. I haven't spoken to him since he shot me."

"I was glad to hear that you survived. I thought you were going to bleed out that night."

"Thank God I didn't."

"Who would have known our lives would have changed the way it did?"

"No one does, that's what makes life unpredictable."

"That's true."

"But I better go. It was good seeing you."

"Likewise."

He stared at me before walking past me and going to the clothing store nearby. I shook my head again, not believing what I just heard. I knew in the back of my mind that something was going on with those two, but I didn't want to believe it. I took a deep breath and went to my car. At least now I knew what type of person Tyrik is. Regardless, it made me see that he wasn't the one for me anyway. I was trying to deny the feelings I had with Damon by being with him. I'm glad things turned out the way it did and I'm with the man that I always wanted to be with.

Damon

After leaving the house, I was feeling really guilty for lying to Zuri. I wanted to tell her where I was going, but I couldn't. I didn't want any issues to erupt if I did.

After an hour of driving, I stopped my car in the parking lot of the United States Penitentiary in Beaumont, looking ahead at the building, wondering if I should get out. I took several deep breaths before turning off the ignition and opening the door. I went through the doors as I had to go through the protocol of being checked before entering. I later gave my ID to the clerk as he directed me to the visitor's area. I walked in and went to where the clerk instructed. I waited for a few minutes until the doors on the other side opened and my uncle walked in. I glanced at him, still not knowing why I was there to see him. This man has done so much to me and my family that I should let him rot, but to a certain extent, I felt I should see him. He raised me and taught me the rights and wrongs of life. For that, I kind of do owe him that much.

I waited until he sat down before I picked up my phone on my end. He picked up his and gave a small smile.

"Hi, Damon. I didn't think you would come to see me."

"I wasn't going to."

"Why did you?"

"Because regardless of what you have done, you're still my uncle."

He sighed. "Did you tell Zuri you were coming?"

"That's not any of your concern. So, what did you want to tell me?"

"I didn't think I would be telling you this here, but I guess I don't have a choice."

"What is it, Julian?"

"It's about Milo. I know you and Zuri killed him."

I gave him a smug look. "How would you know? You've been locked up."

"People do talk in here, D. Malcolm has some people on the outside and they know for a fact that you two staged his apparent suicide. If that's what people are calling it."

"He doesn't have proof."

"He can get it, especially since there are video cameras around the hospital. If I was you, I would take Zuri and DJ and leave."

"Wait, this is the first day I'm talking to you since you were arrested, so how do you know I have a son?"

"Just know that people are watching you, even when you don't think they are."

I didn't say anything else as I got up and went to the door. For all I know, this could have been a set-up to get me out of the house for Malcolm to do something. I should have known just because he's in prison he could still do things behind bars.

"Damon! Please don't do anything crazy."

I turned around and stared at him. I tried to go back when the guard told me I had to go.

"If this was a set-up, I swear I will come back and kill your ass!"

The guard was ushering me out as I stared at Julian. His face was a mixture of fear and anger as I shrugged the guard off of me. I walked past him, grabbed my ID from the front and headed to my car. I immediately called Zuri, seeing if she was there with DJ. I needed to hear her voice so she could take our son and go somewhere else. But there was no point in running. I was tired of that. We need to settle this once and for all.

I stopped killing once I became a family man. Now, in order to protect my family, I will go back to doing it again.

***

I sped back to my house, almost causing two accidents on the way while coming off the freeway. The hour and an hour drive felt like twenty minutes as I kept calling Zuri. I haven't been able to get in touch with her for the past thirty minutes, which was making me worried. After calling three times in a row, she finally answered with annoyance in her voice.

"Damn, baby, what's the emergency?"

"Are you at home?"

"No, but I'm about to go back. What's wrong?"

"Is DJ with you?"

"No, my parents are watching him. What is going on, Damon?"

"Call them to see if they're okay. I'm heading there now."

"Damon, what is going on?"

"Just do it, Zuri!"

I hung up and threw the phone in the passenger seat. I started praying, hoping that what Julian said was a lie and that everyone was safe. Twenty minutes later and Zuri and I were pulling up at the same time. We both got out of our cars and went to the door.

"What the fuck is going on, Damon?"

I put my hand over her mouth when I noticed a black SUV sitting on the corner of the street. If it was for us, I didn't need anything to trigger them.

"Don't say anything," I whispered in her ear as I looked to the windows. I made sure nothing was out of place as I pulled out my gun from my waistband. I was still a cop, so of course I had guns stashed in my home and in the car. I just kept them in places I knew DJ couldn't get to since he's starting to walk now.

"You have yours?" I whispered to Zuri. She nodded as she opened her purse and grabbed her gun out. Since what happened, Zuri has become a pro at firing a gun. I'd taken her to the gun ranges around town and purchased her a gun. With our history, we have to be on alert at all times, so the practice came in handy.

I really didn't want to do this, especially if DJ is in the house. Hopefully Clyde and Daphne took him to their house, but they would be in danger regardless.

I motioned for Zuri to open the door, which she did. If this was two years ago, she would have been nervous to be involved in this, but this is all second nature to her now. I guess she's been around me too long.

We slowly walked in, guns in place, as I walked in front of Zuri. I didn't want to turn on any lights, but it was dark as hell, so I had to follow the light from the windows. We walked into the living room and saw Zuri's parents tied up. She ran over to them as I looked around for DJ.

"Where's DJ?" Zuri asked while untying her mom.

"They took him."

"Who did?"

"Looking for someone."

We looked up and saw Malcolm holding onto DJ, which literally made me lose my shit. I tried to go over to him, but I was met with the backhand of one of his men. I fell down on the hardwood floor, feeling the effect from my throat as I started choking.

“Bitch ass! That’s what you get for trying to fuck with me and mine. You locked my ass up and killed my brother, who was also your damn dad! What type of son are you to do that to your father?”

Zuri went over to me, but I waved my hand at her. She didn’t have to worry about me. I got this.

"How did you get out of prison? You were locked away for life?” Zuri asked.

“That’s the beauty of having money. You can pay anyone off with the right amount.”

“Mommy, daddy!” DJ yelled. The sound of his voice made me regain my strength as I got up and went over to Malcolm. His men tried to get to me again, but shots from Zuri’s gun went off, hitting one of them in the back. She fired another shot at the second man, hitting him in the chest. I heard screams from Daphne as I aimed my gun at Malcolm.

"Now, you have two options. You can hand over my son and you’re going back to prison, or I can shoot you right where you stand. Take your pick?”

“You wouldn’t do that with your son right here, would you? You’re just like your dad if you do.”

“Let him go, Malcolm!” Zuri yelled.

“Aww Zuri, Zuri, Zuri. I saw your little interaction with my son earlier. How he explained that Iesha is his child and that Erin is her mother. That part is true. That little hoe was sleeping with both of us and we didn’t even know. Anyway, at one point, I thought that little girl was mine. Thank God I dodged a bullet on that one.”

I looked at Zuri, still on the fact that she spoke with Tyrik. Although this wasn't the time to be upset, she could have told me she did.

"Where are you going with this, Malcolm?" Zuri asked.

"You put too much trust in my son, Zuri. How else would I have known anything about you two while I was in prison? Yes, I have men on the outside, but who was the one who put all of this in motion for me?"

I looked at Zuri, who gave a wide-eyed expression. I guess Tyrik really wasn't to be trusted.

"But why? You shot him?"

"Yes, I did, but in order to keep that little girl safe, he had to do what he needed to do. You two should know that. I mean, look at this little boy. He's an innocent little thing. Too bad his parents aren't so innocent."

"Leave our son out of this!" I yelled.

"And what are you going to do about it, nephew? Kill me like you did your dad!"

"If that's what it takes, then I will!"

"I'll have you both locked up for Milo's murder. Don't think I can't do it."

"How, when you're the one who's supposed to be? Now, I'm not going to say it again, hand over our son, now!"

Malcolm pulled out his gun and aimed it at me. "You want me to put another bullet in you, because I'll be glad to do it."

"You know what, I don't have time for the games. Either you shoot me or don't," I said. I gave him a convincing look as he held DJ tighter. He started to cry even more, which made me want to shoot him, but I knew I couldn't since he still had my son.

"Please, Malcolm, just let our son go. What if that was Tyrik? How would you feel about that?"

"I wouldn't have any problems shooting him again. He betrayed me once, so he'll do it again."

I had to do something. I couldn't continue watching him holding my son. I slowly tiptoed over to the door while Zuri distracted Malcolm. I looked over at Clyde and Daphne and put a finger to my lips so they wouldn't speak. Zuri was trying to keep Malcolm focused on her as I continued walking. I got behind him as Zuri continued talking. He put DJ down, which was good for what I was about to do. He went over to Zuri as I pulled my arm out and put him in a chokehold, causing him to become unbalanced. Zuri quickly gave DJ to her parents as I still had Malcolm in a chokehold.

"Get DJ out of here!" Zuri exclaimed to her parents as I was still fighting with Malcolm.

He struggled himself off of me and smiled. "You want a fight, then come on, nephew. Let's see what you can do without that damn gun."

"Gladly. I can kill you with either a gun or my bare hands. Either way, after tonight, you won't be bothering me or my family again."

I looked at him as he tried to punch me. I blocked his hit and gave him an upper cut against his jaw. He tried to hit me again, but I drop kicked him, putting him down on the floor. It would have been easy to get my gun and shoot him, but I think I have done enough shooting for a while.

Malcolm looked at me and smiled. "You still a weak ass, like your damn adoptive father. He let so many men run through his wife, it was a shame. Which posed the question, is Milo really your father?"

I looked at him as the door swung open and the police rushed in. Zuri grabbed a pair of handcuffs and threw them at me. I caught them and slapped them on his wrists.

While I read him his rights, I picked him up and stared into his eyes. He still had that smug look on his face, which I wanted so bad to punch the shit out of him.

“I really hope this time your charges will stick and you rot your ass in prison. Get this piece of shit out of my house,” I said to one of the officers as I shoved him to the door.

“Son of a bitch. Where the hell were you guys? I called you an hour ago,” I asked Ramirez as he came to me. He was recently promoted to Sergeant, which I honestly don't see how he was.

“We had to see if he had any other men around your house, which he didn’t.”

“That doesn’t mean anything. He could still try and come after us again while he's in prison,” Zuri said.

“He won’t. We uncovered some of his hiding spots where several of his men are housed. They were arrested and are in police custody.”

“What about Tyrik?” I asked.

“Actually, Tyrik was a part of the plan. He was wired when he was talking to you, Zuri. We had to do it in order for him to tell us his whereabouts since Malcolm contacted him. Sorry we didn’t tell you.”

“It would have been nice if you would have informed us. Hell, this is our house!” Zuri exclaimed.

Sergeant Ramirez sighed. “I can’t believe I have both of you on the force to deal with. Just know that we will do everything in our power to lock O’Neal behind bars for good.”

“Let’s hope so.”

"But good job you two. We’re going to need you both down at the station for your paperwork.”

"Of course," I said.

As soon as Ramirez left, I looked at Zuri and smiled. "He's right, you held your own Detective Baxter."

"Thanks, and of course, you did too."

"I always do, in everything that I do."

"Oh really."

"Yes, and I'll prove that to you later in the bedroom."

I smiled while she shook her head. "I don't think we'll be staying here tonight."

"Since this is still our anniversary, we can get a room, stay holed up in there without any interruptions and have as much fun as we want."

"Hmmm, counting on it."

We were about to kiss when we heard someone clear their throat.

"Yes, Dad," Zuri said without even looking.

"What is this about you being a cop? When did that happen?"

"What about your event planning business?" Daphne asked while holding DJ.

"I went into the academy after I had DJ. I was recently promoted to detective a month ago. As for my business, I can run that as well as be a detective. Damon does it with teaching."

"You put her up to this, didn't you?" Clyde asked me.

"This was all on her, Clyde."

"After what I had experienced, I realized I wanted to do something worthwhile with my life besides planning parties. Instead, I want to be able to change our communities and I think being with the force will help me do that."

"Well, we're proud of you, honey. Aren't we, Clyde?"

He looked at Zuri and sighed. "I guess. I don't like the idea, but if it's what makes you happy."

"Thank you."

"As for your anniversary, go spend it. Make us another grandbaby," Daphne said and smiled.

"Oh, that's definitely the plan tonight," I said, making Zuri blush. I looked at Clyde who looked pissed off and I shrugged.

"So is this what being involved with you consists of? Us always being tied up by thugs?" Clyde asked.

I shook my head. "No, hopefully this will be the end of it."

"Unless we make more enemies, so you should probably keep an open mind," Zuri said.

Clyde rolled his eyes and Daphne took him over near the couch.

I looked at Zuri and sighed. "Some anniversary."

"It's fine, baby. I'm just glad Malcolm will really be put away."

"That's true. But before all of this, there was another assignment we were given."

"And what is that?"

"I think it would be better to show you than tell you."

She smiled and came over to me and gave me a kiss. We pulled away as we watched one of the men being wheeled off on a gurney.

"Do you think we can move?"

"That's a possibility," I said and kissed her again.

One thing about Zuri and me is that through the ups and downs we have found a way to stay together. I know now that whatever we'll face, we both know that we will both be by each other's side for the ride.

Zuri

A month later after the fiasco with Malcolm, Damon and I were back on our grind with our normal routine as a business owner and professor and our jobs as detectives. The two of us have discussed our second lives, wondering if we should end it and actually continue on with our normal lives. At least we wouldn't be fighting off criminals or putting ourselves in danger, but honestly, it's sort of a thrill to do what we do and to help get criminals off the streets. It's a win-win for us. Hell, I'm even thinking about going into the FBI, but that means I would have to leave my family for periods at a time, and I don't know if I could do that.

Since we didn't get to celebrate our anniversary, I figured this was the perfect time to plan a nice evening for Damon. That, and I have a surprise for him that I think he will enjoy.

So much was going through my mind as I stared at a picture of the two of us on our wedding day. I still think about that day and how happy we were. The ceremony was beautiful and it was perfect for the two of us.

While my parents have DJ for the night, Nicole was at my house getting me ready. She looked at my face and smiled. "You look beautiful, Z."

"Thanks, girl. I don't know why I'm so nervous."

"You shouldn't be. You and Damon have been together for practically forever now. You two have dodged bullets, jumped off cliffs, and were almost killed by two crime bosses. If that hasn't tested your relationship, then I don't know what will."

I smiled. "It's not that, it's just that the two of us are finally settling into things now and now I'm going to spring this on him."

"Trust me, Z, he'll be happy."

I sighed. At least we know now that Malcolm is locked away in a maximum security prison where he can't escape. As for Julian, he's also serving life in prison for not only murdering Chandler, but also being an accessory to kidnapping, murder, and extortion. I'm sure those two will die in prison, which wasn't a bad thing.

"I just want to make things better for him, especially since he did that paternity test with Malcolm."

When Malcolm mentioned he was also involved with his mother, Damon became curious and requested a paternity test on himself and Malcolm. After days of waiting and wondering, the test did reveal that Malcolm was not his father. Although it was still bad that Milo was Damon's father, at least I can be relieved to know that I didn't sleep with two brothers.

"You know that would have been awkward if Damon turned out to be Malcolm's son, but it's still kind of weird that you were involved with the two."

"It is, but at least they're not blood related."

"Besides that day, do you still talk to Tyrik?"

I shook my head. "No, but I did read online that he got married to Christette, which I'm happy about. Everyone deserves a bit of happiness in their lives."

"That's true. Take me for instance. Even though I still love Chandler, I was able to open my heart again to be with Malik. I still can't believe he has changed."

"You and me both, but I'm glad he did."

"I was also surprised at how he took to Cole. You know how some men can be with being around another man's child, but he's great with him and Cole loves to be around him."

"How is Cole adjusting to not seeing Chandler? I remember you telling me he was having a hard time with it."

Nicole sat for a few minutes without saying a word. I knew she was trying to get her thoughts together without breaking down. That's something we have both done when we talk about Chandler.

"He's still adjusting. You would think at his age that he probably wouldn't understand that his dad is not here, but Cole is a bright little boy and so observant. He asked one day where was his dad, which literally tore me apart. It's going to be hard to explain to him why his dad is not here."

"His death was senseless, just like all the other incidents that have occurred. Thank God that things are slowly coming into place."

Nicole nodded. "Yes, they are. At least Julian and Malcolm are both behind bars where they belong."

I nodded. "I still hate what those two put Damon through, especially Julian. The man raised him to be the person that he is today, yet he was pulling the wool over his eyes for some time."

"Like they always say, sometimes things are not what they seem."

"Don't I know it."

"But you don't have that to worry about. Now, you and Damon are living the good life and continuing your thrill seeking days by being cops, which I still can't believe that you are."

"Well, people can change."

"I know and the experience you had will definitely change your mind on being one."

She smiled and I stood up, smoothing down my blue and white mini dress, which was also the outfit that I had on the first night I met Damon. It took me two months to fit back into this dress, which I didn't mind, but I sure missed my burgers, fries, and ice cream. Even

Damon was questioning what I was doing. Now, I kind of wish I didn't go on that diet.

"I still can't believe you kept that dress. I threw out all of my clothes from the early 2000s," Nicole mentioned.

"I couldn't get rid of this dress, especially since I met Damon in it. Besides, I wanted to recreate the moment when we first met, so I had to dress the part."

"I see why Damon wanted to bone you on the first night."

"Well, he can any night, day, or afternoon that he wants to," I said and winked.

"I bet, you little hoe."

I laughed and grabbed my clutch from the bed. "I really hope you have fun, and don't worry about D. He's going to love it." Nicole said.

I nodded and Nicole gave me a hug before we both went to the hallway. I took a deep breath, hoping that tonight would turn out the way I wanted it to.

***

After going through traffic, I was standing outside of the club where we first met, which was now turned into a concert venue. I watched as a crowd was forming, which made me think about when Nicole and I were waiting in line and Damon caught my eye. A smile formed on my lips as I felt him near me.

"Recreating the first night we met. I like that."

I looked behind me and I smiled. He was wearing the same outfit that he wore that night. Who knew we could both be sentimental?

"I figured we should go back to how it began."

"So, will the night end the same as before?"

I smiled. "Definitely, except I won't sneak out in the morning."

"You better not."

He took me away from the venue and we walked away, thinking we were going to the diner next door, but instead, he led me to the fusion restaurant across the street. Once we walked in, he confirmed a reservation, and I smiled.

"You're not the only one who can do surprises."

"I'm loving this one," I said as he pulled out my chair. I sat down as he went to his.

"So, Mrs. Baxter, is there any other surprises you have in store for tonight?"

"Maybe one or two."

"Are they good ones?"

"I believe they are."

As the waiter came over with the wine list, Damon asked if I wanted anything, but I waved my hand no. He gave me a curious look and I pulled out the entrée menu.

"What gives? You always order wine."

"This time I'm not. Just changing things up."

"You sure nothing is up?"

"Nothing is up, baby."

I stared at him while he was looking at the door. I turned around, wondering what he was staring at. Donte Foster, the guy that we've been tailing for the past month, just walked in with someone other than his wife. He's a key suspect in embezzlement with the company he works for. We're still trying to get the proof together, but we know he's guilty.

Damon looked at me and shook his head. "It looks like our celebration will be cut short. Again."

"It doesn't have to be. He might not even pull anything."

"You want to bet on that? When he does, you're going to have to dance for me tonight. And I want the full effect, baby."

"That's not a bet. I would do that anyway, unless if I'm right, you'll have to dance for me."

Damon smiled. "That's a bet."

We watched as he was in a deep conversation with the female. They looked over at another table at a couple who was giving them mean stares when the man put his hand underneath the table.

Damon groaned. "Fuck."

Both men were about to stand up and pull out their guns when Damon and I drew ours first.

"H.P.D., put down your weapons, now!"

Diners nearby began to go underneath their tables as we moved closer to the men. The other guy pulled his down and I went over to handcuff him. Of course, Donte had to be the difficult one and had his still aimed at Damon.

"Of course you had to be difficult. I'm trying to have a night out with my wife and you're ruining it."

"Like I give a shit!" Donte yelled.

"You'll give a shit once you're arrested. Now put down your weapon!"

I sat the guy down when I noticed Donte's female partner was trying to protect her man by pulling out her weapon. I pointed mine at her, which had her startled.

"Don't even think about it."

Donte rolled his eyes, which pissed Damon off.

"What are you mad about? Not only are you stealing money from your company, but as I recall, you also can add attempted murder by trying to kill your boss. Am I right?"

I looked at Damon, wondering if he was telling the truth. There wasn't anything in his profile indicating that.

"That's falsified information. I could sue you and the department for that."

"Go ahead, but you'll be doing it from a jail cell. Now, I'm going to say this one last time, put your weapon down now!"

Donte fired, causing mayhem around the restaurant as his girlfriend tried to come at me. She tried to punch me, but I knocked her on her ass and she slid across the hardwood floor. I grabbed a couple of ties that held the table cloths together to tie her wrists.

"You shouldn't have done that. Now, you're going to jail."

Damon was still trying to control Donte as he tried to go to the door. I stuck my foot out as he tripped and fell onto the floor. Damon came over to him as I grabbed his cuffs and slapped them on Donte's wrists.

"You're a stupid muthafucker, aren't you?" Damon said.

"Fuck you, prick!"

"No thanks, but I'm sure you'll find someone in prison who will."

I shook my head at him as a couple of officers came in. Ramirez looked at us and sighed.

“Wasn’t expecting this, were you?”

“Not at all. Can we have some time alone?” Damon said.

“You know that’s impossible when you’re a detective. But your theory sticks. We got the proof we needed to charge him for embezzlement as well as attempted murder. Throw this in and he’ll be looking at some serious prison time.”

“Hopefully his sidekick too,” I pointed out.

“This is her first offense, so two to three years, tops. But it was good you two were here. Another case closed.”

“Yeah, and another evening ruined. Thank you, Ramirez,” Damon said.

“Glad to be of service.”

Damon gave him the finger and I laughed. “Baby, stop. We still have the entire night.”

“I know, but I just want us to have a night out without having to worry about pulling out our guns or arresting someone. I want us to be normal.”

“What are you saying, that you want out?”

Damon sighed. “I don’t know. Maybe I want to see what else life will bring.”

“Well, if you do quit, then you’ll have some time to be Mr. Mom twice over.”

“Twice over. What are you talking about?”

“I’m pregnant, D.”

He looked from me to my stomach and then at me again. "Really?"

"I just found out today. I won't know how far along I am until my next appointment."

"Wow. Come here," he said and gave me a hug. He held me tight as I breathed a sigh of relief. At one point, I didn't think I wanted to have kids, but now, I love the idea of being a mother, so this was great news for us.

"Before long, we're going to need that minivan."

"Let's not go that far."

He looked at me and smiled. "Who knew how far we would come."

"Yeah, all from a one-night stand."

"But we knew it wasn't going to be just that."

"We did, even though I was too stubborn to admit it."

"You're always like that."

"Whatever."

Damon pulled me closer and whispered in my ear. "You still going to dance for me, right?"

"Is that all you're thinking about?"

"A bet is a bet, so you have to honor it."

"Of course."

"Wear something sexy for me."

"You know it."

He stared into my eyes and smiled. “I love you so much.”

“I love you too.”

Eight years ago, I didn’t expect to meet my husband outside of a club, nor was I expecting my life to be a roller coaster ride. I had so much doubt in our relationship, which led us to grow apart, but I’m glad that Damon didn’t give up on me or us. Now, through all of the ups and downs, we’re happy, with the occasional adventure or two. But regardless of how our life is together, I wouldn’t change it for anything.

Music Playlist

The music playlist for *Love & Drama: The Root Of All Evil* is a great mix of songs that I believe describes the story between Zuri and Damon's journey as they experience everything from love to adventure.

James Brown- The Payback
Chic- My Forbidden Lover
Angie Stone- 2 Bad Habits
Janet Jackson- Unbreakable
Lianne La Havas- Unstoppable
Jack U, Skrillex, Diplo, AlunaGeorge- To U
Calvin Harris & Disciples- How Deep Is Your Love
Travis Scott- Antidote
Tory Lanez- Say It
Bryson Tiller- Don't
X Ambassadors- Renegades
Elle King- Ex's & Oh's
Demi Lovato- Confident
Nick Jonas- Levels
Rudimental & Ed Sheeran- Lay It On Me
The Weeknd- Often
Chris Brown- Back To Sleep
Justine Skye – I'm Yours (feat. Vic Mensa)
Miguel & J. Cole- All I Want Is You
Jeremih- Oui

About the Author

Sheena Binkley first discovered her love for storytelling when writing her first story for a class project at the tender age of nine. Since then, she has composed several short stories and numerous tales that are not only engaging, but simply entertaining. She is also a freelance writer, penning articles on various topics including education and entertainment.

To date, her best-selling novels include *In Love With My Best Friend*, *Love Unbroken*, *Something Just Ain't Right*, and *The Love Chronicles.*

In April of 2016, Sheena launched her own publishing company which focus strictly on romance books. Besides writing, she loves reading, shopping, and spending time with family and friends. She lives in Houston (where the weather is always unpredictable) with her husband and son.

Email: sheenabinkley@live.com
Goodreads: www.goodreads.com/authorSheenaBinkley
Blog: sheenabinkley.wordpress.com/
Facebook: www.facebook.com/sheenabinkleyauthor (Like Page)
Twitter: @ChevonBink
Google +: https://plus.google.com/+sheenabinkley
Pinterest: Sheena Binkley
Group:
https://www.facebook.com/groups/577100099053119/?fref=ts

Made in the USA
Columbia, SC
23 June 2025

59782405R00169